Terror, is this really market, that witnessed

...TON PUBLISHING CORPORATION
Bensalem, Pennsylvania

HOLD BACK THE NIGHT

Sandra Steffen

A KISMET Romance

METEOR PUBLISHING CORPORATION
Bensalem, Pennsylvania

For Ernie, who never ceases to amaze me.

SANDRA STEFFEN

Sandra Steffen grew up in Michigan, surrounded by an extremely large, noisy family where the changing seasons couldn't help but inspire romance. She doesn't know where she acquired her love of books, but remembers happy hours spent reading as a child. That love of reading transformed into a love of writing several years ago. She, her husband and their four school age sons live within miles of that large, noisy family, which has become larger and noisier than ever.

PROLOGUE

May 25, 1943

Hannah stood statue still, the wind tugging at her hair, drying a tear from her cheek as late morning sunshine warmed her hair and shoulders. Gazing across the vast waters of Lake Michigan, she imagined the waves of an ocean instead, imagined the same sun glinting off a man's red hair. Unable to contact him, she prayed for his safety, hoped someday he'd come to understand.

She turned from the lake, letting her gaze drift about the shoreline, settling on the brightly painted lighthouse and stone cottage. Memories of the previous summer echoed on the wind, memories of a man, strong and tall and proud, memories of the love they'd shared, of the life they'd created.

The lighthouse drew her thoughts to the past, just as the short, high-pitched cries of her newborn daughter broke into her reverie, drawing her to her future. Moments later the cries ceased and a loving smile settled to her lips.

She understood her reason for coming here. She'd come to say good-bye. Her fingers smoothed over the small leather-covered book in her hand. Although she knew it would have no place in her new life, she couldn't bring herself to destroy it. Destroying it would be like destroying the love she'd given, the love she'd received. The diary belonged here, with her past, a written legacy of the summer of her seventeenth year.

She hurried over the path and slipped through the lighthouse door, up the wooden stairs where she put the magnificent view to memory. Seconds later she did the same with each of the rooms in the connecting cottage, tucking her diary into a safe, secret place. When she finally pulled the heavy door closed behind her, the sun again warmed her hair and the look in her husband's eyes warmed her saddened heart.

From the stand of pines where he'd stood waiting, he started toward her, meeting her halfway, his limp now barely noticeable. She gently took her sleeping daughter from his strong, capable hands, and they walked side by side to the old truck filled with their belongings. He started the engine and gripped her hand as they pulled away from the Lake Michigan shore. Her daughter's slight weight felt warm against her breast. She squeezed her husband's hand, squeezed her eyes shut, but she didn't look back. Her heart swelled with love for the man at her side, for the child in her arms, for the man on the ocean so far away, a love that would forever bind them together, a love she knew in her heart would never die.

ONE

The car slowed, creeping steadily over the bumpy road that had been reduced to little more than a cow path the past several years. The road, beyond the intersection he'd passed a mile back, was no longer used. It was simply a bumpy lane that connected the village main street and the old lighthouse on Lake Michigan's east shore.

A weathered No Trespassing sign was nailed to the dilapidated gate. Another was fastened over the doorway that led to the lighthouse tower. He chose to ignore both.

The April breeze blew the scent of fresh water inland from the Great Lake. The breeze was unusually warm for northern Michigan in mid April. Just yesterday he'd overheard two men talking about the record that had been set last year and the snow that had blanketed the landscape before melting away, finally relinquishing its wintry hold on the area.

He didn't know about any records. He'd been in

the area a few short days and frankly, as his eyes scanned the circular tower, its white paint peeling from years of cruel winds and neglect, he didn't care about any records. At least not records concerning the weather.

He slid his hands into his pockets and circled the structure. This was it. He could practically taste it. The building was exactly as his grandfather, or— he grimaced—the man he'd always thought was his grandfather, had described.

With long, powerful strides he followed an old path around the weathered structure. All his life, he'd been drawn to lighthouses. Strange for someone growing up inland, miles and miles from even a river of any considerable size.

This lighthouse was connected to a sturdy stone cottage. Rattling the knob, he found the cottage door bolted against intruders. As he continued to investigate the property, fallen twigs and pine needles cushioned his footsteps. He automatically surveyed the surrounding area for any movement, then walked to where the cottage joined the lighthouse. He stopped for a moment, deep in thought, then continued around to the other side.

With his head tipped back, he squinted into the bright sunlight. The tower extended forty feet into the air, and he had a sudden driving need to behold the view from that height. The door leading to the cottage faced the lane. But the lighthouse door faced Lake Michigan. A single lock, not terribly sturdy, attempted to keep intruders out.

Even with the higher than normal April temperatures, the wind blowing off the lake suddenly turned cool. Goose bumps rose on his flesh, and a shiver snaked down the length of his spine. He didn't shudder because of the cold. His hide had withstood worse. He felt the shiver because he somehow sensed that here, somewhere in this very structure, he'd find his answers.

Hunching down, his eyes level with the heavy lock, he removed the thin, pointed strip of steel from his pocket. With painstaking patience, he worked the steel into the lock, until he heard, as well as felt, a definite *click*.

He straightened to relieve the muscles in his thighs from their uncomfortable position, then slid the picklock back into his pocket. He ignored the knot in his gut as he gripped the doorknob. The heavy door swung open without a sound.

He stopped, suddenly alert. Something wasn't right. His eyes narrowed as he scanned the interior. From the light streaming through the open door, he saw footprints on the old, dusty floor. Men's footprints.

It wasn't until after the door had shut without so much as a whisper that he realized what was wrong. He'd expected the heavy old door to open with a groaning creak, the hinges stiff from years of idleness. Instead they hadn't made a sound.

He touched his sturdy fingers to the rusted metal of those old hinges. Bringing his fingers into the light he sniffed the shiny moistness coating their tips.

Oil.

Who would oil those hinges? This was private property. Of course, that hadn't kept him out. But who would care whether the door creaked or not?

Someone who didn't want to be heard. That's who.

Questions for which he might never find an answer filled his mind. Questions not only about oiled hinges, but also questions about where he came from. And where he was going.

He wandered about the ground floor of the circular chamber, his footsteps increasing their pace, his mind willing the structure to whisper the truth of his questionable heritage. Although he felt the possibilities hovering just beyond his reach, the very air in the lighthouse maintained its muted silence.

You're losing your grip. Lighthouses can't talk. There had to be another way to learn the truth about that long-ago summer. If there was a way, he'd find it. It was that simple. And that complex.

With long, muscular strides, he took the spiraling stairs three at a time, turning after he'd reached each landing, until he entered the upper chamber.

Starr Davison's eyes drank in the sight of the old lighthouse looming in the distance. As she neared, her lungs expanded with the moist air blowing off the Great Lake. Her weariness and tired muscles were completely forgotten as she reached into the pocket of her jacket for the old black key. A moment later the lock gave way.

She turned the rusted handle, then leaned her shoulder against the heavy frame. The cottage door slowly creaked open. Her eyes widened, then gradually became accustomed to the dim interior. Leaving the door open, Starr roamed about the cottage.

She'd come home.

She imagined the lighthouse as her uncle had described it, when it had been in use decades ago, marigolds blooming by the back step, the lighthouse painted a pristine white, its glass polished, the cottage spotless, so different from its appearance today. Dust had gathered in layers on every surface—on the rustic woodwork, on the old furniture, on the ancient tiled floors. The dust didn't matter. What her homesick heart craved even more than the sight of the cottage was the view from the top of the old lighthouse.

Starr walked to the door that connected the cottage to the lighthouse. After turning the lock, she opened the door. The hinges squeaked sorely. She began to climb the wooden spiraling stairs, her sneakered feet thudding on every step.

A distant *creak* invaded his thoughts. He drew his eyebrows down in concentration. Straining his ears, he listened, suddenly alert, for another sound. After a few moments, another totally different sounding *creak* followed from below. Then, the thud of muffled footsteps, sure and even, could be heard as someone began to climb the stairs.

Who would be interested in this old lighthouse? Who, besides himself, that is? Maybe the same person who had oiled those hinges. Maybe the person who didn't want to be heard.

No. Whoever was coming up those stairs didn't care who heard. This person had used the other entrance. The creaking door had alerted him of his entry.

With watchful eyes, he surveyed the circular structure, searching for a place to hide. He found no such place. With silent footsteps, he positioned himself to the right of the stairs, just in case he'd find it necessary to make a hasty exit.

Barely breathing, he remained perfectly still. Blending in with the curved walls, he watched as the intruder emerged from the stairwell. His eyes narrowed, and in an instant he realized the intruder was a woman. He soundlessly expelled the breath he'd been holding, but his eyes never wavered from her.

The woman exhaled loudly as if her legs were opposed to the uphill climb. She squinted against the light pouring in through the glass windows facing Lake Michigan. As the April sunshine twinkled through airborne dust particles, he watched a smile tug at her full lips.

When she moved, he again held his breath. Without noticing his presence, she walked to the vast windows, her head slowly moving as her eyes swept over the abundant marine blue of the lake.

Just as slowly, the woman turned to face him. Surprise widened her eyes as it narrowed his.

He knew the exact moment fear replaced the surprise in her eyes. She sucked in a half breath of air. Yet she didn't scream. She watched him as intently as he watched her. "What are you doing here?"

His brows rose slightly. He hadn't expected the tartness of her voice. There was a time when his face would have remained completely in control, his expression giving nothing away. He was aware of the change in him. Those changes hadn't been easy to accept. But he was also aware that he didn't have to tell this woman anything he didn't want her to know.

"What are *you* doing here?" he countered.

Instead of answering his question, she demanded an answer to another. "Who are you?"

He didn't reply.

The fear didn't leave her eyes, it just moved over to make room for her anger. "How did you get in here?"

"How did you get in here?" he asked in return.

He watched her gaze dart about the room. He was standing near the stairway, making her escape impossible. The look in her round hazel eyes told him what her words wouldn't. She was afraid of him. She probably thought he was a murderer or rapist. The fact that she hadn't panicked told him even more. She was going to try to find a way to outmaneuver him.

She leveled her gaze to his and blurted, "All right. I'll go first. You want to know how I got in here? I unlocked the door with a key. Now it's your turn."

If he hadn't been listening for it, he wouldn't have heard the slight quake in her voice. She was gutsy, he'd give her that much. How many women in these circumstances would stand up to a stranger? Her bravery surprised him. He'd expected her to be afraid, anxious, even hysterical. God knows he'd seen enough hysteria to last a lifetime. Ten lifetimes.

With a voice that equaled hers in tartness, he said, "What makes you think I don't have a key too?"

One side of his mouth rose the tiniest bit, almost as if he wanted to smile. As Starr noted the change, a portion of her fear subsided. Fortunately, she was able to maintain the hold she had on her emotions.

"Not a chance," she returned. There were only two keys. She had one in her pocket. The other hung from the key holder in Uncle Mick's kitchen.

"Ah." The stranger shrugged, his gesture one of complete nonchalance, as if to say, Oh well, it was worth a shot.

Starr watched his every move. As he slid his hands into his pockets, a shiver started at the back of her neck, then crawled all the way down her spine. Did he have a weapon concealed in his pockets? A gun? Or a knife?

Without speaking, the man took a step toward her. In the same instant, as if moving to some silent dance, she took a step back. Three times, they repeated the maneuver.

He pulled his left hand from his pocket, then held his empty hand, palm up, in a gesture of innocence. "Look, lady, I don't have a gun. My only weapon is a picklock."

Her eyes widened, as fright, stark and vivid, shivered in their depths. Her breath caught in her throat as the man pulled his right hand from his pocket. A partially empty crinkled brown wrapper filled his palm.

She thrust her chin up at the sight of the candy wrapper. The fact that he liked chocolate didn't make him less dangerous. He'd broken into her lighthouse. She intended to find out why. "Who are you? And why did you pick the lock to get in here? What are you? A thief?"

"I'm not a thief."

"No? You pick locks and break and enter, but you're not a thief. Oh, that's believable," she said, sounding like she didn't believe a word of it. "If you didn't intend to steal something from the lighthouse, why are you here?"

For the first time, his eyes left her face. Starr watched as his gaze strayed over the curving interior of the lighthouse, then beyond to the point where the pale blue sky met the deeper blue of Lake Michigan.

Without speaking, he walked toward her. This time she held her ground as he neared. His legs carried him closer to the vast windows. He seemed to be trying to form a reply.

Starr continued to keep him in her sight as he walked past, turning first her head and then her entire body. He still didn't answer her question. Instead he stood, silently staring into the blue distance.

From her position several feet behind him, she watched the stranger. Who was he? Her mind began plucking possibilities from thin air. He'd broken into the lighthouse, yet he'd made no move to harm her. It was too early for the tourist season. So, what was he doing here?

His back was to her and the stairs were within easy access. Now was her chance to flee. Only she no longer sensed danger. At least, not physical danger.

He stood. Tall. Unmoving. The shoulders beneath his bomber jacket were broad. His hips were lean, his legs muscular. What was he thinking? What did he see?

Starr approached the windows, then looked out over the gently rolling waves of the lake. "It takes your breath away, doesn't it?"

Her tone of voice made the question rhetorical. It pulled his gaze from the view. Instead of meeting his look she continued to stare out across Lake Michigan. From his position a few feet from her, he studied her face.

She had a strong profile, feminine, definitely feminine, but strong. Her eyes followed the landscape as she turned her head in his direction, still looking far into the distance. This angle gave him a better view of her face. Her cheekbones were high, her nose straight. Her large hazel eyes, almost gray beneath the dark sweep of her lashes, looked dreamily at the horizon.

Her light brown hair was in total disarray—from the April breeze or from a hairstylist's clever hands, he couldn't tell. With the bright sun streaming through the windows, light touched the airy brown tendrils with golden bronze. It waved in every direction, from the tip of her head, over her shoulders, all the way down to the middle of her back.

His gaze returned to her face, then traveled down over her body. At some point she'd removed her bright red jacket; the sleeves were tied around her waist. She wore a washed-out yellow tee shirt, the Say Yes to Michigan logo stretching smoothly over her full breasts.

His idle fingers flexed inside his jacket pockets as he imagined touching the soft flesh beneath that tee shirt. He yanked his eyes away. But staring at the swelling waves in the distance didn't remove the sudden heat from his body.

No way. There's no way you're going to get involved with a woman. Any woman. Remember why you came.

"I've visited lighthouses all along the East Coast, but I've never found one that could hold a candle to the view from right here. Maybe it's because this is home."

Some of the tartness had left her voice. And in its place, he heard the warmth of affection. "Did you grow up around here?" he asked.

"Yes. And I've been away too long."

"Your family must be glad you're back."

Her voice went soft as she said, "I'm visiting my uncle. He means the world to me."

His mouth clamped shut, his jaw set. Two people had meant the world to him, one old, the other young. Jake and Jazz. Now it didn't matter. They were both dead.

She must have seen the look in his eyes because her next words were spoken in a softer voice. "If you aren't here to steal something, why are you here?"

"Here in this town in general? Or here in this lighthouse in particular?" He contemplated not answering either question.

She held his look, then took a long, deep breath. "Take your pick." It was obvious she wasn't expecting a reply to either.

He surprised himself by answering. "I'm looking for something."

"Have you found what you're looking for?" she asked.

Unseeing, he stared past her at the thick old windows and silent walls. "I'm hot on the trail."

His gaze focused once more as he watched her draw her chin up. "Well, you'd better enjoy the view because I'm going to have the lock changed. Uncle Mick doesn't like strangers in his lighthouse."

"Uncle Mick?"

"Yes." She raised her eyes to his, as if daring him to deny her statement.

The reality of who this woman was hit him like a bolt of lightning. His heart began to thud more heavily. He wanted to ply her with questions. But this wasn't the right time. He'd waited four long months to begin looking. Another few days wouldn't change the final outcome.

He shrugged, then turned away, his gaze sweeping over the marvelous view once more. Without uttering another word he squared his shoulders. With long strides he walked to the stairs.

Starr watched him go. His dark brown hair, which had been subtly streaked with hues of auburn by the sun's rays, was cut short around his ears and forehead. The back, left long, curled along his collar. Before he began the winding descent, he turned to her. His eyebrows were drawn downward, as if he were thinking thoughts he'd rather not think.

"I'm not a thief, you know."

She'd relied on instinct countless times in the past, times when dying patients needed to know the truth, times when sick children needed a reassuring smile. But her instincts didn't help her now. She didn't know what to say to this stranger.

A moment later he was gone.

She was left staring at the place he'd been. Dust particles twinkled through the air as she listened to his steadily descending footsteps. The footsteps paused for a moment and silence filled her ears. Then the door clattered shut.

Starr turned her attention back to the horizon but her mind refused to reminisce. Instead, her brain was filled with questions. About the stranger.

Her homecoming hadn't turned out as she'd planned. Instead of feeling refreshed by spending time in her secret place, her mind was clouded with more questions. She'd wanted to think of Uncle Mick, to remember her childhood. But Uncle Mick's image kept interchanging with the stranger's.

Starr clenched her teeth as she slowly descended the stairs. At the bottom she spied one tiny brown M & M resting on the last step. She bent down to pick up the candy, wondering how it had dropped from his pocket.

Starr was thoughtful as she touched her fingertip to the smooth coating of a dark brown M & M. Her mind once again conjured up the image of brown eyes, squinting into the distance. Chocolate brown eyes. Looking at the candy, she was reminded of the way those brown eyes had melted away her fear.

Although she was almost certain she'd never seen the man before, there was something familiar about his eyes. How could that be? Starr was deep in thought as she locked the doors and began the walk to the old county hospital on the village outskirts.

Twenty minutes later she pushed through the wide hospital door, her lips lifting in a smile of approval at the sight of Uncle Mick. The blinds had been pulled completely up to allow the last rays of the sun total access to the small room. The pane now acted as a mirror against the darkness outside.

He'd fallen asleep seated in a high-backed chair. A small radio played on the bedside table. Mick's ears had probably been tuned to the weather report for *his* lake. From this angle, it was nearly impossible to tell he'd ever suffered a stroke. The doctors had assured her the stroke wasn't as serious as some. Still, his left arm and leg were weakened.

Starr tiptoed into the room and Mick's snore was cut off in mid rumble as he jerked awake. He smiled the moment he noticed her, his eyes crinkling at each corner. Deep grooves slitted the sides of his face as he said, "Come here, lass, and let me have a look at you."

She was twenty-seven years old, but Starr knew if she lived to be a hundred, she'd never grow tired of Mick's nickname for her. *Lass*. She hurried to him, then leaned down to press an emotion-filled kiss on his lined cheek. He hugged her awkwardly and she grinned at the memories his hug evoked. While she would have loved to linger, she knew he'd feel uncomfortable with more than a quick peck on the cheek.

She pulled away, then smiled into the old buckskin brown of Mick Mahoney's eyes. "What are they forecasting over our lake, Uncle Mick?"

"They're calling for clear skies for the next few days. Then a warm front's moving in."

Starr sat at the edge of a chair opposite her uncle. Reaching for his hands, she placed both of hers in his. The skin of his thick, large palms felt dry against the smoothness of hers. Squeezing his hands, she asked, "Do you think *they*'ll be right this time?"

"Hard to say. She's a perplexing mystery, the weather. Almost as unpredictable as a woman."

Starr felt his hands tighten around hers. His right hand was strong. The left one, though weakened, also moved against hers. "You're getting stronger, Uncle Mick."

"Of course I'm gettin' stronger. You didn't think I'd be lettin' this thing beat me now, did you? How was your drive up? When did you get home? And, lass, what have you done to your hair?"

For the first time in three weeks Starr felt her worries fade away. There wasn't another soul on earth who could make her feel the way Uncle Mick did.

She grinned at him and declared, "The drive was long. I arrived an hour ago. And what I've done to my hair cost a pretty penny."

"Hmmph! Looks like you were caught in a whirlwind. Looked better straight. Lass, you're skinny. Don't you eat in the city?"

Starr knew how she looked. She had a head of hair most women would die for. And she wasn't skinny. Thin, for she'd lost a few pounds these past weeks, worrying about Uncle Mick and working double shifts at the hospital so she could come home.

Frankly, she loved her wild-haired look. She wasn't hurt by Mick's lack of tact. Every abrupt word was laced with love.

"I see having a stroke hasn't weakened your temperament. You liked my hair better straight? I'll have to make a note of that."

"Hmmph! You'll make a note, but you won't change it, if I know you." Starr smiled into his crinkled brown eyes. He knew her well.

With a serious note uncommon to Mick Mahoney, he said, "I'm glad you're home, lass."

Her eyes scanned his familiar face. Behind the sprightly eyes, she saw weariness. Beneath his weathered wrinkles, she saw worry. She decided now wasn't a good time to tell him about the intruder in their lighthouse.

Mick watched her closely and Starr held his look, waiting for him to speak. After a moment of serious thought, he began. "I want you to do something for me."

She stared gravely into his eyes, sensing his disquiet. Something in his manner worried her. "What is it, Uncle Mick?"

"A letter arrived last week." He gestured to the drawer near the bed. "I want you to read it." His voice quaked, his words began to slur. A feeling of dread dropped to the pit of her stomach. She reached into the drawer, then took a sheet of paper from its envelope. Forcing her eyes to the barely legible handwriting, she began to read.

The letter was simply written, concise, straight to the point. It was from a man named Shane Wells, a man from Chicago. A man claiming to be Mick's grandson.

Words of denial sprang to Starr's mind. When she looked into Mick's eyes, she couldn't utter them. "You think he's your grandson?"

"I don't know. That's why I want you to find the truth."

"But it's *possible*, Uncle Mick?" she whispered.

"Anything's possible, lass."

Starr was caught off guard. His simple statement shocked her, but the tenderness in her uncle's expression halted her reply. Find the truth? Could he really believe this man named Shane Wells was his grandson?

"I'd do it myself if I was out of here. If you won't, then it'll have to wait until I'm strong again. . . ."

Mick was tiring. With his fatigue, she noticed the pronounced slur in his speech. Starr's eyes rested on his weathered but still handsome features. She'd never forget the kindness he'd bestowed upon her the day her parents drowned. His was the first face she'd seen. She'd had no living relatives and Mick Mahoney, her father's old and dear friend, had taken her into his home, comforted her in her loss, and raised her as his own daughter.

He'd never asked anything of her before. She couldn't deny him now. Starr's heart seemed to have lodged at the base of her throat. She squeezed both his hands once more. "I'll try, Uncle Mick," she promised over the choking beat of her heart. "I'll try."

The following morning Starr was up with the sun. After wandering about her uncle's quiet house, she set off on a vigorous hike, hoping the exercise would clear her mind.

Uncle Mick was her only *family*, but he wasn't really her uncle. They weren't blood related, but she couldn't have loved him more if they were. Mick loved her, too. She knew in her heart it was true. But there had been moments throughout the years when she'd glimpsed a deep yearning as he stood gazing out over the waters of Lake Michigan. In those moments her heart had swelled with worry that Mick felt a void she couldn't fill.

What if that void had been for a family? A *real* family. A grandson was *real* family.

"Starr Davison! If you aren't a sight for sore eyes."

Starr had barely realized her steps had brought her here, into Maybell's Food Mart at the edge of town. She was abruptly caught around her waist and unceremoniously hugged against the rounded girth of Maybell Atkinson's full bosom. The hug was over as quickly as it began, and Starr couldn't help but smile down into the crinkled blue eyes.

"May, it's good to see you, too."

"When did you get home?"

Starr loved the sound of that. *Home*. "Last night. What's new in Pinesburg, May?"

For the next several minutes she listened to Maybell's version of village news. Before long Starr knew that old Jed Harrington had a hip replaced, Stella Randall was expecting twins, little Tina Cambell had a crush on Maybell's grandson, Rusty. Barely stopping for a breath, May said, "Tell me, Starr, how's that cantankerous uncle of yours feeling?"

"He's getting stronger—"

Starr blinked as Maybell interrupted her. "Went up to see him myself just the other day. Stubborn as a mule, that one. But strong as one, too. He'll make it back. He's too gawdblain ornery to be sick for long."

Murmuring her agreement, Starr tossed her hair behind her shoulders. Inside, she felt the strain of the past three weeks, the long shifts at the hospital, the burning need to come home. Now that Mick had asked for her help, a cold knot had formed in her stomach.

The bell jingled over the door, signaling the arrival of another customer. Starr's gaze automatically turned at the sound. Silently, she watched as a man rounded the first aisle and strode straight to the candy counter. The stranger from the lighthouse.

After making his selection, he turned, placed some change on the counter, then strode from the store the same way he'd entered. He was tall. And big. Yet he moved without a sound. The knot in Starr's stomach grew.

He stopped in mid stride and, tipping his head

back, emptied a portion of the M & Ms into his mouth. A craving for chocolate crept over Starr and her mouth watered as she imagined the smooth, sweet flavor of those little candies. Without a backward glance, the man resumed his long strides until he rounded a corner and was out of sight.

"Is there something I can help you find, Starr?" May's words drew Starr's gaze from the empty doorway.

Hurrying to the candy counter, she searched for her favorite little chocolates. She scanned the wrappers of other kinds of candy. "Are you out of M & Ms, May?"

Maybell leaned down to examine the bottom shelf. "Well, I'll be. I knew we were getting low. I guess that newcomer beat you to the last package. I can't seem to keep enough chocolate on the shelves these days. Seems everyone's turned into a chocoholic."

"Who's the newcomer?" Starr asked.

May turned her white, curly-topped head to glance across the store at her other customers. "Don't know his name. Quiet fellow. Keeps to himself. Came in day before yesterday. Bought some frozen dinners and a handful of chocolate candy. You can tell a lot about a person by the food he buys."

Maybell's gaze flickered to her other customers. Clicking her tongue, she sputtered, "I'd better go help those two young folks. Stop by again, Starr. Real soon."

Starr watched Maybell's white head bob away, barely visible over the top of the next aisle. She smiled in spite of herself. Some things never changed.

Pausing a moment, she looked around her. The

old store had changed little since she'd last seen it. The same aging shelves supported row upon row of grocery items. Scuffed from the feet of decades of shoppers, the slightly uneven oak floor was still the same indescribable brown. Scents of spices and tobacco mingled in the somewhat musty air just as she remembered.

Nothing had changed. The sense of permanence surrounding this store, this town, filled her heart. This was her hometown. Uncle Mick was the closest she had to family. He was all she had. She'd find the truth about that man down in Illinois. After all, the chance that he *actually* was Mick's grandson was next to nil.

Pushing through the old door, Starr headed west, her steps following the gradual decline of the narrow sidewalk, over familiar, quiet streets. She didn't have to think. Her feet knew the way. She'd go back to the place she'd always gone. To think, to plan, to remember. Starr Davison had come home.

TWO

It took Shane only a matter of minutes to drive from the lighthouse back to his rented cabin. But then, he hadn't exactly paid attention to the speed limit. He entered his cabin and without bothering to remove his jacket walked directly to the old brown couch. Lowering his frame to a sitting position, he picked up the sheaf of papers lying against the worn cushion.

His second visit to the lighthouse had uncovered even less information than the first. He stared at the evidence held tightly in his hand. Evidence. It was nothing more than hearsay. Descriptive phrases, dates, names, and places, all written in his own barely legible handwriting, could hardly be classified as evidence.

He'd come across nothing but snags from the beginning. Jake had taken the answers to all Shane's questions with him to his grave. What did he really have? Mumbled memories of a dying man.

Jake. Wherever Shane's thoughts took him, they always returned to Jake. His eyes clung to the scribbled words jutting across the papers he held so tightly in his hands, analyzing, constantly analyzing the meaning behind those jumbled memories. With a sudden power, he jolted to his feet. He thrust the now crinkled sheets of paper to the old, sturdy couch. With his muscles flexed, his fingers curled into fists at his side.

With the soundless footsteps of a man familiar with stalking lowly serpents in dark alleys and decrepit buildings, Shane prowled about the sparse interior of the cabin. He came to an abrupt stop, his eyes blind to the scenery beyond the window. Instead, his vision was fixed on a scene within his memory, a scene that had taken place over four months ago.

"Your mother knew. But it never mattered to her. I was always going to tell you, too, Shane, when the time was right."

The rasping words brought Shane's eyes from the hospital parking lot far below to the old man resting sedately against white sheets. The room smelled of disinfectant. It smelled of impending death. It wouldn't be long, and then his grandfather Jake would be gone.

"You're like him, you know."

Shane's eyes met his grandfather's. "I'm like who, Jake?" He had called his grandfather by his first name for as long as he could remember.

"You're like Mick. Your mother, she was the spitting image of your grandma, Hannah. My Hannah."

Shane's eyebrows drew downward. What was Jake talking about?

"Right from the beginning, Kate was like her mamma. I looked for a resemblance to Mick. But all I ever saw was Hannah."

Resemblance to Mick? Who in the hell was Mick?

"I told your mamma. When she was old enough, I told her. Know what she said, Shane?"

"What did she say, Jake?" Shane didn't know if Jake was talking out of his head or not. What he was saying didn't make sense.

"She said I raised her. That made me her father. Kate. So much like her mother, my Hannah."

Jake's eyes had taken on a glassy sheen. He was tiring from the exertion of talking, but still he continued. "My Hannah. I still remember the way her pale gold hair blew like satin on the Lake Michigan breeze that summer. I loved her. So did Mick."

The old man halted his speech, trying in vain to catch his breath before continuing. "Hannah loved us both, you know. Not at first. At first she had eyes only for Mick. But then, with your mother on the way and Mick gone off to war, she came to me. And she grew to love me. She did. She loved us both."

"Jake, try to rest." Shane's voice was etched with a deep rooted emotion. Anguish. Memories of his father were vague, memories of his mother sweet. Both had died when Shane was small, first his father, then five years later, his mother. It was his grandfather, Jake, who had raised him. Now he, too, was dying. Jake was the only family he had, and when he was gone, Shane would be alone.

But the old man wouldn't rest. Not until he'd relieved his chest of its heavy, aged burden. "I've never been sorry. Never. Watching Kate, so much like Hannah, grow . . . I couldn't have loved her more if she'd have come from my own flesh. Never been sorry.''

A lump formed in Shane's throat, swelling until he thought he couldn't breathe. He wished Jake would rest. The end was near. He could feel it. It hovered nearby, waiting. Waiting.

"Hannah died when your mamma was but a wee lass. . . .'' The old man's eyes took on a twinkle as he continued. "*Wee lass*. I haven't used that phrase in a long time. Mick. He spoke with a Scottish lilt without even thinkin'. His mother was Scottish, his father a proud Irishman, you know.''

No, Shane didn't know. He didn't have any idea what Jake was talking about. But as Jake continued, questions began to strum through Shane's head. In his own roundabout way, Jake was trying to tell Shane something.

Jake's eyes darkened with remorse. "I've always wondered how Mick reacted when he came back from the war. Mick was a keeper of the lights, you know. We did what we had to do, Hannah and I. Never meant Mick any harm. I can still see his red hair glinting in the sunshine, polishing the glass or painting that old lighthouse.''

Shane's eyes had narrowed as he tried to follow the jumbled train of Jake's thoughts. Whatever it was, it had to do with the past. It had to do with his grandmother. And his mother. And someone named Mick.

The old man was lost in his memories for a moment. With shallow breaths, he tried to continue. But he was growing weaker. Before Shane's eyes, Jake was slipping away.

Jake's next words were spoken over the rasp of

his labored breathing. "You're like him, you know. Your mamma was like Hannah. And you . . . you're like Mick. But ya see, Shane, it never mattered. Your mamma was my little girl. And you're the son I never had."

Shane grasped his grandfather's arm, saying, "Jake, rest now. We can talk later. Rest."

"Yep, right from the beginning, you had a lot of Mick in you. You know your own mind. And you live your life on the edge. I can still see Mick keeping his lighthouse shipshape. He was always ready to rescue ships wrecked in winter storms. Like you, he thrived on the edge. Ah, Mick, good old Mick . . . so much like you, Shane."

Gradually, the swelling buds swaying on the branches of otherwise bare trees came into focus. A slow ache burned within him. Shane squinted his eyes against the pain. Loneliness. Now that Jake was gone, it invaded his chest like a dagger thrust in the dark of night.

For more than four months he'd lived with the dagger of being alone. Before Jake had died, Shane had been able to keep his inner self separate from what he did for a living. But after Jake's death and all Shane's unanswered questions, the rancid smell of crime and death had pierced his armor, just as a bullet had pierced the heart of the boy he had been trying to reach. Jazz was a street kid, street smart and street tough. Given another chance, he could have made it out. But Jazz had run out of chances.

Shane had been deathly close to running out of them, too.

Death. It had steadily circled, then surrounded

him. His grandmother, his father, his mother, Jake. He'd dealt with it every day in his work, as well. Until it took that brave kid. Jazz's death had been the final straw.

Through the whiskered clump of faraway bushes, Shane saw a patch of red advancing toward him. It was a woman. Even from this distance, his practiced eye discerned that much. As the woman trudged nearer, the wind lifted long strands of her light brown hair, swirling the ends behind her.

It wasn't just any woman. It was the woman. The woman from the lighthouse. The woman who had been raised by Mick Mahoney. Even though Shane didn't smile, the lines in his forehead disappeared. As silent as the wind, he slipped out the side door.

During the first mile resentment forced the strained muscles in her legs to carry her over the uneven gravel of the bumpy lane. But her resentment had fizzled out a half mile back. Now Starr simply concentrated on putting one foot in front of the other.

She'd overdone it. The muscles in her legs screamed it with each step. Her racing heart and weary breathing begged for a break. Instead of resting, she pushed on.

Up ahead, Starr saw the Kearn cabin. Its shutters were opened and a shiny silver car sat in the driveway. It was a little early for vacationers and she wondered who was living there now.

There was a time when she would have known who was staying in the Kearn cabin. She would have been aware of every incident, rumored or otherwise, taking place in the village. In that instant, Starr felt it more clearly than ever before. She'd been away too long. And now, more than ever, it was good to be home. It would be even better when she could fall across her old bed, rest her tired legs, maybe even close her eyes for a few minutes.

One, two, three, four. One, two, three, four. She counted each step.

I can take a long, luxurious nap as soon as I get home. She was nearing the Kearn cabin. *After all this exercise, I've earned something sinfully rich for dessert.* Her mind pondered the possibilities. *A hot fudge sundae. Chocolate brownies. Boston cream pie smothered in fudge sauce.*

Her mouth began to water and the walking became easier. Without conscious thought her steps slowed. What was it? What had she seen? Or sensed? There had been no movement.

He didn't move a muscle. The brown of his jacket blended perfectly with the weathered trunk of the old maple tree. Only his eyes moved. He'd watched as she neared. She looked neither right nor left, her thoughts, it seemed, far away.

She'd moistened her full lips as she trudged on. And as he witnessed the gliding motion of her pink tongue whisking over her smooth full lips, his stomach lurched. A sensuous throb descended to the lower half of his body.

His mind, as well as his body, was completely aware of the feeling. For the second time in as many days something other than the numbing fingers of loneliness uncurled in his gut.

Without reason, her steps slowed. Then stopped. He watched as she turned to face him. Her large, hazel eyes locked with his.

How had she known he was there? Beneath his calm façade, he felt the prickling fingers of unease. Then the unease ebbed. Adrenaline surged beneath the surface of his skin. His blood heated all the right places and he read the silent challenge in her look.

Just as silently, he accepted the challenge. For the first time in a long time, a smile threatened to tip his lips. "How did you know I was watching you?"

Holding his look, she said, "I just knew."

He recognized the tartness of her voice. "What kind of an answer is that?"

"Why were you watching me?"

"Men have been watching beautiful women since the dawn of time."

His feeble compliment failed to move Starr, but his voice once again nearly melted her senses. That voice could have belonged to the devil himself, so rich and smooth, so full of hidden meaning. Or it could have belonged to a hero.

Even though he stood some distance away, leaning with deceptive calm against a tree, a slow heat crawled up her body. It was a heat that had nothing to do with his trite line. It had to do with the stranger.

The devil, she decided. And like the devil, something about his broad shoulders, something about the gleam in his eyes, something about the way the wind combed through the auburn streaks in his hair tempted her.

He may have had the aura of a devil, but he had the face of a hero. He had eyes that saw too much, a nose that could sniff out trouble, the shadowed stubble on a beard-roughened chin, and a mouth . . . Starr allowed her gaze to rest on the firm line of his lips. His mouth was honest-to-goodness sensuous. She had yet to see it lift into a smile.

Part of her wanted to see him smile, wanted to take him in just as she'd taken in countless stray kittens when she was a child. Another part of her wanted to turn and run. If he made one move to come near her, that's exactly what she'd do.

"How long have you been living in the Kearn cabin?"

Crossing one foot over the other, the stranger settled himself more comfortably against the tree. "About a week. How long have you been back in town?"

Her eyes widened. Back in town? How had he known she'd come *back* to town?

She didn't hesitate to throw him a rivaling question. "Will you be staying long?"

"I haven't decided. How long will you stay?"

Once again he wasn't telling her much. Her eyes searched his. "I haven't decided," she replied, mimicking his reply word for word.

His lips parted. It obviously wasn't the answer he'd expected. She didn't move an inch as his gaze narrowed on hers. His chest expanded as he sucked in a quick breath.

Without further conversation, Starr turned back toward the country road. Not far ahead, the gravel gave way to asphalt and the road turned into a village street. After the brief rest, she practically groaned out loud as she pushed her legs on, trying not to limp. One, two, three, four. She counted her steps.

One, two, three—that man could inspire the lyrics of a love song—four.

One, two—maybe he's not the devil after all—three, four.

One—but then again, maybe he is—two, three, four.

"I could give you a ride."

Her steps halted as she considered his offer. Starr turned to face him once again, measuring him with her look. Her instincts told her he wouldn't hurt her. For now, she'd rely on those instincts. "I'd appreciate that."

"Wait right there. I'll bring the car to you."

With silent fascination, Starr watched his every move. He ran with the grace of the April breeze. He moved, long limbed and muscular, with the inborn splendor of a hero.

Or a devil.

Sand and gravel spun beneath the tires as the man put his foot to the accelerator. His car skidded to a stop a few feet from where Starr stood, battling with her good sense. *He didn't attack me earlier in the lighthouse. He's harmless.*

Harmless. Maybe he wouldn't *harm* her. But that didn't mean he was harmless.

Leaning down, Starr studied him through the car window. If harming her had been his intention, he could have done it in the lighthouse. Or right here. Once again, she sensed that he wouldn't hurt her. At least not physically.

Leaning across the seat, the man opened the door. "Climb in." His gaze held hers. Was it a challenge? Or a plea?

Starr slid onto the passenger seat. He immediately gunned the engine, the lurching momentum throwing her head back against the upholstery. With one fluid motion, she clicked her seat belt tightly around her.

She turned to view his profile. A groove peeked out from the side of his mouth. Had he almost smiled?

"Where to?"

"To my uncle's house on Elm Street. On the other side of the village. You may want to take the long way around."

His eyes left the road to look at her face. "Why?"

"If you stay on this street, you'll drive smack past the police station."

The groove beside his mouth deepened. There was no denying it. His mouth stretched into a full-fledged grin. A tiny place deep inside her responded to that brief smile. Starr grasped the armrest to keep her balance as the stranger sped around a corner. Without a word, he bypassed the police station.

The way his lips had been briefly overtaken with his open smile disarmed her. The whiteness of his teeth, the amused angle of his strong chin, and the deep chuckle that blended with the roar of his car's engine sent Starr's pulses racing.

With the skill of a stunt driver, he whisked the car around another corner. The grooves beside his mouth were still pronounced even though his smile had slipped away.

In record time, he pulled up along the curb of her uncle's house, turned in his seat, and looked at her. Never in her life had a man looked at her the way this stranger did at this moment. Starr wanted to make a run for the house the minute he shifted the lever into park. His driving bordered on reckless.

Yet she didn't feel afraid. He seemed in complete control.

That was what bothered Starr: his controlled recklessness. She had to get out of there. Without a word, she released the seat belt and flung the door open.

His fingers clamped around her wrist. Maybe her instincts hadn't been correct after all. She drew in a short breath as her eyes automatically traveled to the hand barring her exit. Those fingers curling around her wrist had an iron grip. Yet the pressure against her skin felt oddly possessive.

Panic darted inside her. She felt the power beneath the firm grip of his fingers. If he chose not to let her go . . . Blinking once, Starr's gaze slid from his hand to the magnetic sheen of his clear brown eyes. He had leaned closer, his face now a scant six inches from hers. The scent of woodsy aftershave clung to his chin, blending with the freshness of the April breeze which seemed to be the very essence of the man himself.

Her eyes were locked with his for but a moment, yet Starr was certain she'd glimpsed the edge of an unspoken, unforgettable pain. He wasn't a man crazed with evil ideas. She was certain he was a man who'd suffered, truly suffered, some searing emotional pain.

Her panic subsided. Her awareness didn't.

His nearness affected her breathing. His unknown aura caused her heart to thud in a more pronounced rhythm. Starr held her breath, suddenly wondering what his mouth would feel like blending with hers.

Her lashes swept down against her sun-kissed cheeks. When her eyes flew to his he found himself drowning in the liquid smoke of her look. He was aware of the riot of her wind-tousled hair defying direction around her face. But his eyes didn't leave hers.

He loosened his grip around her wrist, felt the vein pressed beneath his finger pulse a heady rhythm. She was affected by their closeness. Her attraction drew him, excited him.

The hours and the wind had stripped her face of makeup. Her skin looked smooth and soft. His gaze touched upon the softly curving bow of her lips. Such a kissable mouth.

She didn't move. Neither did he. Something held him back. He wanted to. Oh, how he wanted to . . . to feel her soft lips move beneath his. He came close, so close, to saying to hell with his own code of ethics and kissing her the way he longed to kiss her. Instead, he clamped his mouth shut and withdrew.

He knew who this woman was. Regardless of the fact that he hadn't felt this much reaction in a long time, he also knew that if he acted on these feelings, she'd feel deceived when she discovered his identity.

Damn. Deception is what had brought him here in the first place. Swallowing his desire for her, he moved back into his own bucket seat. He stroked his finger in a smooth half circle along her jumping pulse one more time. With tremendous reluctance, he pulled his hand from her slender wrist, then dropped his palm along the length of his right thigh.

His retreat back to the driver's side of the car startled her. For a moment, his finger had caressed the sensitive skin at her wrist. Her skin still tingled from the pressure of his thumb.

Starr had been so sure he was about to kiss her.

His restraint surprised her, disappointed her. But only for a moment. Then irritation settled in. His touch excited her. But her reaction to that touch aggravated her. Starr didn't take chances with safety. She didn't accept rides from strangers. She didn't wish, if only for a moment, to feel that stranger's mouth pressed to her soft lips.

Or did she?

He didn't speak. And neither did she. With as much grace as she could muster, which she doubted was much since the overtired muscles in her legs had turned to putty, Starr slid from the passenger seat. After hurling the door shut with a loud slam, she started up the sidewalk.

"The least you could do is thank me for the ride."

The cadence of his voice stopped her in her tracks. Starr placed her hands on her hips, then turned to face him.

With the door gaping open, he stood beside his car, one arm resting comfortably along the roof. Even though his statement was spoken like a command, his eyes held amusement. His expression was oddly soft and gentle.

Her gaze locked with his and some unknown longing settled in her heart. A knot rose in her throat. It was the way she felt when a dying child climbed into her lap. Warm and full. And sad. Because she knew that something precious was coming to an end.

She couldn't explain why this stranger's smile evoked such feelings, but this time she could protect herself from the hurt. As long as she didn't succumb to the warmth in his eyes, she'd be safe.

This was the third time the stranger had gotten the better of her. If he thought she was going to thank him for driving like a bat out of hell, he could think again!

"Thank you? The next time I'll walk! You drive like a maniac!"

Light flashed in his eyes. A moment later he began to laugh. Those first chuckles sounded slow and creaky, as if he hadn't laughed in a long, long time. Starr was reminded of reluctant gears being prodded back into use. The sound built until his laughter flowed easily, if not naturally.

"That's what you get when you accept rides from strangers."

When he laughed, years melted from his face. His eyes twinkled with sensuality. And the lines in his forehead disappeared. It was a sound Starr felt drawn to. Like temptation. Just hearing his creaky chuckle tipped her own mouth into a silken grin. It somehow helped to restore her dignity. And mystify her at the same time.

"You're definitely strange. What's your name anyway?"

"What's yours?"

They were back to that. All right, she'd go first. "Starr Davison." She held his look, daring him to tell her his name. Or daring him not to.

"Shane Wells," he stated, his voice touched with a unique mixture of pride and obstinacy.

The grin drained from her face. Her heart thudded in her chest. For a moment her gaze faltered. She raised her eyes to study the man watching her from the street. Shane Wells, her intruder and stranger all rolled into one.

Shane Wells. The man claiming to be Uncle Mick's sole surviving relative.

Perhaps she couldn't protect herself from hurt after all. But he didn't know that. Her voice dropped lower, ingrained with as much strength as she could muster. "I've been expecting you." *But not yet. Not for a long time.*

She knew the pleasure had slipped from her face. She couldn't help it that her voice had gone from friendly to suspicious, like a person taking measures to protect her property from potential burglars.

His eyes glittered with some unnameable emotion. "I told you before, Starr, I'm no thief."

Her gaze never wavered from his. She raised her chin and squared her shoulders. "Yes, I know what you said. I hope you get exactly what you deserve."

The way she said it made it clear she thought he deserved to be tarred and feathered. Or skinned alive. Or worse.

THREE

"Joanna! Let me look at you." Starr's worries retreated to some far corner of her brain the moment her friend entered the restaurant. Jenny, Joanna's three-year-old daughter, looked with fascination at Starr's waving hair, then shyly hid behind her mother.

Patting her protruding waistline, Joanna said, "This is all of me."

"You look beautiful," Starr proclaimed. And she meant it. Joanna's dress billowed out around her. "You look positively radiant."

"You sound like David. He used to tell me I was sexy. Now I'm radiant. I've had enough radiance. I want to look sexy again."

Starr's gaze softened on her friend. "When's junior here due?"

Joanna made a face, puffing her cheeks out and widening her eyes. "One more month." And Starr said a silent prayer of thanks for finding such a friend in Joanna.

While Joanna helped her daughter to sit, Starr said, "Hello, Jennifer. The last time I saw you, you were just learning to walk. Look at you now. You're so grown-up!"

"I know. This is the women's night out, you know," the little girl said, mimicking the words her mother had spoken to Jenny's father earlier.

The waitress came to take their orders. And the two friends talked and reminisced, seated in the old family-owned restaurant located in the first block of the village main street.

What the restaurant lacked in ambience, it more than made up for with the home-cooked goodness of its simple cuisine. Starr didn't notice any lack of ambience. What she did notice was the feeling of being where she belonged. The restaurant was a part of the town. The town was the place where she'd grown up. And, until last night, she'd taken it all for granted, as if it were all rightfully hers. The town, the people, her place in Mick's life.

Not anymore. Her sense of home was intricately woven around her uncle. He'd needed her. And she'd needed him. Only now there was someone, a man by the name of Shane Wells, who claimed a much stronger tie to Mick Mahoney than she.

Starr pushed those thoughts away and tried to concentrate on Joanna. They were barely into their main course when Maybell Atkinson's voice interrupted them from the doorway. "Why, look over here, girls, it's Starr, Joanna, and little Jenny."

"Oh-oh, here comes the town's chief gossip and her three ranking followers."

"Joanna!" Starr hushed her friend.

"Starr," Maybell gushed, "I was just telling the

girls here that you're back in town to take care of Mick."

The "girls," looking as alike as sisters with their matching white hair, red-painted lips, brightly flowered blouses, and dark knit slacks, attested to this statement.

"Jenny has her father's eyes, don't ya think?"

Before Starr could answer, one of the others predicted the exact date Joanna's baby would arrive. There wasn't much Starr could add to that.

"You're so thin," Maybell clucked.

Starr wasn't expecting the kick in the shin from underneath the table. "She wouldn't be talking about me," Joanna sputtered.

Maybell patted Joanna's shoulder. "Nonsense! Why, you look lovely, Joanna. And you're not fat. Why, no, that's just baby fat."

Starr was laughing out loud by the time the "girls" had echoed their agreement and retreated to their own table by the windows smack dab in the front of the restaurant.

Joanna rolled her eyes and shook her head. "You can laugh. You don't have to put up with everyone in this town knowing every single thing you do or say," Joanna exclaimed.

Jenny pulled on Starr's sleeve. "Daddy says Mommy gets cranky like this because her back hurts on account of the baby." Starr laughed again and Joanna continued to shake her head.

The dregs of his third cup of strong coffee had cooled in the white mug. The middle-aged waitress was chatting with a customer at the other end of the room, and Shane didn't want to call attention to himself.

Half hidden behind the old support beam and an artificial potted plant, he silently watched Starr. His meal had been properly seasoned and adequately cooked. It very well could have tasted wonderful. Shane hadn't the slightest idea. Eating had quieted the rumbling in his stomach. But his attention had been fastened on the woman across the room, his eyes beholding her every move.

She had an exquisite neck, cream colored and smooth looking, especially where it curved to join her shoulders. Her hair lay in tumbled waves against the jade green of her blouse. The dim rays from the overhead lamps sent shimmers of light dancing along the airy tendrils, the light changing her brown hair to gold.

Shane wondered what had inspired her parents to choose her name. Starr. The name suited her. Her features were as alluring as starlight.

As a child, he had stood in his backyard, reaching his hands to the sky. He'd stretched his fingers, trying to touch the stars' twinkling beams of light. How he'd yearned to hold the elusive starlight in the palm of his small hand.

Watching her now, he felt the same yearning to reach out his hand and touch her, somehow connect with her. *Shane, you've been too long without a woman.* As he clenched his jaw, he realized that, until now, he hadn't cared.

He told himself he watched her to gain insight into the mystery of his possible parentage. Or grandparentage. But he felt his body's reaction to her warm smile. He found he wasn't immune to the way she tilted her head when she listened to the little girl. He wanted to sift his fingers into the chaotic strands of her hair. But it was an elusive want, as elusive as catching starlight.

People stopped by her table to say hello. The affection the villagers felt toward her was obvious. In return, her feelings for them appeared genuine. This was definitely her hometown.

Shane felt very much an outsider.

Placing her water glass to her lips, Starr was aware of a disquieting feeling rustling within her. She'd felt it all through dinner. At first she'd blamed it on hunger. Her plate was now empty, her hunger satisfied. Yet the feeling remained.

Jenny, it seemed, had had enough of acting ladylike. The little girl proceeded to climb, first to her knees and then to her feet, until she was standing on the seat of her chair, swaying, it seemed, to some lyrical tune in her imagination.

After several attempts to calm the child, Joanna cast an apologetic glance at Starr. "I'd better get her home. When she starts dancing, the table is apt to fall down."

Starr withstood her friend's worried stare. She knew Joanna saw something in her eyes, troubles Starr didn't want to talk about. Her friend's gaze softened as she murmured, "When you're ready to tell me about it, I'll listen."

Starr reached her arms to hug her friend. And as Joanna's rounded girth pushed against Starr's flat stomach, Starr felt a definite kick from within. Leaning away, she said, "Junior just kicked me."

She didn't utter another word. And Joanna laughed

aloud at the expression on her face. Reaching her small hand up to rest along her mother's stomach, Jenny said, "That's our baby. We don't know if it's gonna be a wrestler or a ballerina. But it sure can kick!"

Lowering to her knees, Starr smiled at the little girl. "You have a lucky mommy."

"Aren't you going to have any babies, Starr?"

"I don't know, sweetheart. How about a hug?" That uneasy feeling was back. Starr knew it didn't have anything to do with Jenny's question. She knew one didn't need to have children to feel complete. Completeness didn't come from what you had. It came from within. And right then, the feeling coming from within was not one of completeness. It was a vague feeling. One she couldn't identify. It was . . . strange.

Standing alone near the table, she watched until Joanna and Jenny were out the door. Visiting hours at the small county hospital didn't start for another half hour. And after her exercise that afternoon, she'd promised herself something sinfully rich for dessert.

With her thoughts a jumbled mixture of her friend, her uncle, and the man she'd met earlier, Starr sat down at the table. "Dottie, would you bring me the dessert menu?" she called. Maybe that vague feeling within her was a craving for chocolate. Or maybe it was another kind of craving altogether.

There was just something about her. She looked soft all over, from her hair to her smile. But he'd seen her backbone straighten; she was no pushover.

There was something else. Like him, she looked lonely.

Unlike him, she wasn't the least bit reluctant to draw attention to herself. From this distance, he couldn't quite hear the words being exchanged between the waitress and Starr Davison. Her expressions were slightly obscured by soft lamplight.

He watched her study the menu, her brow crinkled in concentrated deliberation. After a moment she handed the menu to the waitress, who then hurried away to the kitchen. In a matter of minutes, the woman was back, a smile on her round face and a delicious looking dessert in her hand.

Raising his mug to his mouth, he sipped the cooled coffee with distaste. He lowered the mug to the table, the bitter taste lingering in his mouth completely forgotten.

Across the room Starr plucked a bright red strawberry from its cloud of whipped cream and fudge sauce. Holding the stem between her thumb and forefinger, she opened her mouth, then slowly sank her even teeth into the juicy fruit. She closed her eyes in rapture, her tongue slowly licking the thick, sweet fudge sauce from her lips.

His brow furrowed as heat shot to his midsection. His gaze remained fixed on her face, as, taking the spoon in her hand, she slowly, so slowly, began the ritual of savoring her next nibble.

Watching Starr enjoy the simple pleasure of indulging in dessert sent a smoldering heat flaring out to his limbs. As an intensity coursed through him, his pulse quickened. Something deep within him was coming to life, pulling at his insides.

With the second berry, a dollop of whipped cream

rested on the fullness of her bottom lip. Her pink tongue flicked, from one corner of her mouth to the other.

Shane's mouth watered. But not for a taste of the luscious dessert. He ached to taste the richness of her soft mouth. It was a sudden ache, one that surprised him with its bluntness. As his gaze lingered on her lips, he was tempted.

As soon as that first sweet strawberry swirled over her taste buds, Starr's eyelids fluttered down, her lashes resting along the curve of her cheeks. If walking those miles enabled her to indulge in such succulent sweets, she'd never give it up.

With deliberate slowness, she ate on with near-sinful relish. All through dinner she'd been aware of a vague sensuous sensation lurking along the perimeter of her consciousness. The sensation had hovered over her, tingling at her pulse points, tickling her willpower.

Though she'd given in to temptation and ordered this dessert, that vague sensuousness hadn't been appeased. After relishing the first several bites, she felt the sensuousness of the atmosphere more strongly than ever. A sleepy contentedness pulled at her lids as Starr slid another strawberry onto her spoon. While she held her spoon in the air midway between the plate and her lips, her eyes roamed about the room. With an unconscious slowness, her gaze settled into the shadows of the farthest corner.

For one heartbeat her gaze had slipped over him then back again. Her lashes flew up and her eyes widened with surprise as she stared into the shadowed eyes of Shane Wells. The air had somehow seeped from her lungs and Starr had to remind herself to breathe.

She suddenly understood the strange sensuousness that had surrounded her all through dinner. He'd been watching her. The knowledge detonated the heat of some inner storm deep in Starr's body. With her heart pounding, she finally understood her body's yearning. As incredibly delicious as her dessert had been, her body had felt his gaze. And his look awoke another kind of craving altogether.

With careful deliberation, Starr lowered her spoon to her plate. Her mouth had suddenly gone dry. Without taking her eyes from Shane's, she brought her water glass to her lips, carefully sipping, because in her state of awareness, the last thing she needed was to choke on ice-cold water sliding too quickly down her tight throat.

He hooked one finger beneath the collar of the brown bomber jacket draped on his chair and strode to her table. Even though he was a big man, the floor didn't shake beneath his step.

"Starr."

"Shane. You have an uncanny knack of materializing out of the shadows. If I didn't know better, or if I believed in devils, I'd say you weren't real."

"Oh, I'm real, Starr. Flesh and blood real."

He was real, all right. She'd known that a man by the name of Shane Wells existed. But Starr hadn't expected him to show up, unannounced, uninvited. She also hadn't anticipated the strange aching in her limbs. This ache had nothing to do with her earlier hike. It had to do with something elusive. It had to do with Shane.

From the kitchen, pots and pans banged loudly

against one another. After a moment, the whir of a vacuum cleaner pervaded the air. Except for Dottie, Starr and Shane were alone in the restaurant.

She slid her chair back and slowly rose to her feet. Raising her gaze to his, she was suddenly glad she'd decided to wear heels. It was of utter importance to be on the same level as this man.

Earlier she'd been certain she'd seen pain reflected in his eyes. She looked for it again. But this time his emotions were carefully concealed. A shiver rippled through her. She needed fresh air. She needed to get out of there.

"It's closing time," she said, leaving the appropriate amount of money on the table. She hurried toward the exit. Shane didn't make a sound but she somehow knew he was following.

Out on the sidewalk in front of the café, she took a deep breath, trying to lighten the heaviness centered in her chest. The cool air helped restore her equilibrium, but it didn't alleviate the heaviness in her heart.

"Not a soul in sight," he murmured.

Starr was confused by her unexpected response to his deep voice. She gazed across the sidewalk at him and replied, "I'd forgotten the villagers roll the sidewalks up at eight o'clock."

He looked up and down the dark streets as if categorizing every shadow, every store and alley. "Where I come from, people bolt their doors out of fear. But another kind of life, a lowly form, creeps out of the concrete and lurks in the shadows at night."

"Great. Now I'll be looking over my shoulder for the bogeyman as I walk home tonight." Although crimes could happen anywhere, she wasn't seriously afraid of being harmed here. When she'd first moved to New York, she'd taken a class in self-defense, just to be on the safe side. She'd never needed to use those defense tactics, but she felt safer knowing them.

Starr shivered. Goose bumps seemed to climb up and down her spine every time she saw Shane. Not the creepy kind of goose bumps, the kind she felt when she saw a horror movie. These goose bumps were entirely different. These were sensuous shivers.

"I'd be happy to give you a ride home." His deep-timbred voice cut through her thoughts.

"In your car? Are you kidding?" She took a step back.

"I didn't mean on my pitchfork."

Starr's gaze flew to his. Her breathing was shallow as she remembered she'd compared him to a devil. He didn't look like a devil tonight. He looked at her seductively and she felt the magnetism between them.

"You made it perfectly clear this afternoon that you didn't like my driving. Whether you believe it or not, Starr, I'm a safe driver."

She couldn't tell him it had nothing to do with his driving. She couldn't tell him she refused to be alone with him because he might be Mick Mahoney's grandson. She wished he wanted something else, anything else. Why did he have to want the only thing she had to cling to?

Shaking her head slowly, she tried to smile. "I've already been subjected to your abominable driving. No thanks. I'll take my chances with the bogey-man." Starr was as surprised as Shane at the faint trace of humor in her voice. She wasn't totally adverse to him. Oh, she didn't believe he was her uncle's grandson. Or at least she didn't want to believe it. But she wasn't unkind.

His expression was utterly serious. She wondered how long it had been since he'd joked his way through simple conversation. For a moment she wondered if he ever had.

"Abominable driving? I drive just like a little old man." His deep voice dissolved her breath away. From out of nowhere a smile played along his lips. It was all she could do to tear her gaze away.

She thought about some of the near misses she'd had when little old men had been behind the wheels of automobiles. "I wouldn't brag about that, Shane. Back in New York, most of my close calls have involved little old men."

"Well, I don't know anything about the men you date. I thought we were talking about my driving."

With the suddenness of his statement, her mouth broke into a wide, open smile. "I didn't date them! I just leave them plenty of room when we share the same highway."

With surprising ease, a smile played at the corners of his mouth. For a moment, Starr was mesmerized by his slow grin. For a moment she forgot who he was. For a moment, she simply enjoyed the surprising humor of the stranger.

"Are you sure I can't give you a ride home?"

"No thanks, Shane. I'm not going home." Starr clamped her mouth shut. She hadn't intended to say that. She didn't want to tell him where she *was* going.

"You're not?" The smile faded as his expression grew serious.

"No. I'm going to the hospital. To see Uncle Mick." She searched his face, trying to read his thoughts. His features were well controlled, but beneath his dark lashes, Starr thought she saw loneliness shade his eyes.

If she'd seen any other emotion, she might have been able to turn away. But not loneliness. Starr understood loneliness. Too well. Too darn well.

"How is he?" Shane's voice was deceptively low.

"He's tough as nails on the outside." With a reassuring voice, she added, "He's going to make it."

There was no masking the relief she saw settle over his features. *Oh, no. The man cared. Why did he have to have feelings? How can I fight someone with a warm heart?*

Shane cleared his throat. "I'm glad. Good night, Starr."

"Shane?"

"Hmmm?" His voice was as smooth as silver moonbeams.

She wanted to say something—to wish him luck, to wish him happiness. But she couldn't. His happiness would be her heartache.

"Never mind. Good night," she answered in barely more than a whisper.

Starr watched him stride down the block to his silver car. He really did move like the wind. She stood there, rooted to the sidewalk, until his taillights rounded the corner at the edge of town.

She inhaled a deep breath. The damp air seemed to seep right through her. She pressed her chin into the collar of her warm full-length coat to ward off the chill of the cool April evening.

With all her heart she wished Shane hadn't come.

She was afraid that, because he had, things would never be the same again. Those thoughts carried her the two blocks to the small county hospital, so different from the huge building where she worked in New York. That hospital was like the city, the halls bustling with activity. This hospital was like the village, quiet, peaceful.

Mick looked up the moment he heard her heels click against the floor. "You're back."

"They couldn't keep me away. You're in a lively mood," she declared.

"Aye. Come in, lass, have a seat, and tell me, how's the view from our tower?"

Starr wasn't surprised he'd asked that question. Of course he'd known she'd go to their lighthouse. It was where she'd always gone. But now, instead of remembering the beauty of the breaking waves of Lake Michigan, in her mind she saw the stranger she'd met in the lighthouse tower. The set of his shoulders, the angle of his chin, the glints in his hair, and the lines in his forehead as he'd watched her added up to a potent image, one that seemed permanently fixed in her mind.

"Have you met him yet?"

There was no use wondering how he knew. "Yes. I didn't know he was in town."

Mick watched her closely. "Maybell mentioned a newcomer. I had a feeling it was him. What does he look like?"

A heaviness settled in her chest as she described Shane. She felt that Uncle Mick was already slipping away from her. Starr lowered her lashes to hide the hurt.

When her uncle grew tired, she kissed his lined

cheek, then hurried from the room. He'd been curious, understandably so. As she wandered through the quiet hospital, Starr's guilt over her hurt feelings only confused her more.

FOUR

Starr walked home from the hospital in the dark, her former mention of the bogeyman failing to scare her now. Instead, her quiet footsteps carried her homeward, her mind spinning in spirals about Mick's request and Shane Wells's untimely intrusion into her life.

She took the key from her pocket, unlocked the back door, and trudged on through the empty house, flipping on light switches along the way. Without stopping, she slipped off her shoes, removed her coat, then walked into the bathroom where she took her robe from a hook behind the door and began to undress. Leaving her clothes where they'd fallen, she wandered through the rooms, lost in thought.

The house was like Mick—old-fashioned, uncluttered, masculine, so different from the places she'd lived with her parents. Starr curled up in Uncle Mick's comfortable recliner. Tucking her feet beneath her robe, she tried to remember what her life had been like with her parents, then smiled at her memories. Her parents had been nonmaterialistic free spirits. They'd believed in peace, in saving the planet during a time when saving the planet wasn't fashionable. When they'd drowned, her sense of security was yanked from her.

Thank goodness the authorities had listened to Mick Mahoney's request for legal guardianship of the child of his dear young friends and neighbors. It had been Uncle Mick who'd handed her sense of security back to her. Now another man was trying to take it away once again.

A rhythmic *drip . . . drop . . . drip . . . drop* penetrated her thoughts. Starr found herself staring at the second hand on Mick's old pocket watch lying on the low table. Every eight seconds another drop echoed through the small house. Every eight seconds. Exactly.

Starr closed her eyes and, leaning her head back, counted *one-Mississippi, two-Mississippi, three-Mississippi . . .*

She tried. With all her might she tried to relax. She squeezed her eyes shut, but they only remained closed from one drip to the next. Exactly eight seconds.

Drip.

With her head tipped back, she found that her eyes were wide open, staring dully at the yellowed ceiling. Some people were relaxed by the sound of water. Not Starr.

Drop.

She was tired, so tired. Her overworked muscles positively relished the soft, cushioned chair. Her body should have felt wonderfully content. It was her mind that refused to relax.

Drip. Drop. Shane. Wells. *Drip. Drop.* Shane. Wells. Her mind turned the steady sound of the dripping faucet into an eight second singsong melody. *Shane Wells* became the lyrics. Releasing a deep breath through pursed lips, she blew wisps of hair away from her forehead. It was no use. Relaxing was out of the question.

What was the matter with her? Why couldn't she keep from thinking about him? He was only a man, for heaven's sake. A thief, no less. But was that true? What if he really was Mick's grandson? Where would that leave her?

She couldn't prevent thoughts of Shane's connection to Uncle Mick from careening through her mind. Standing, she once again felt the sluggishness of her strained muscles. With no real sense of purpose, Starr found herself seated at the edge of the claw-footed bathtub, staring at the tiny drops of water dripping from the faucet. Using all her strength, she tightened the tap. The drip didn't stop. It didn't even slow down. Deeming it useless, she pulled a threadbare towel from the rack to silence the sound. The imagined lyrics stopped.

The house suddenly seemed eerily quiet. She wished Mick were there. But he wasn't. And he needed her help to get on his feet again and to find out if there really was a connection between Shane and him. She wouldn't give up until they had their answers. Starr only hoped it wouldn't mean losing Mick to Shane Wells.

Her bare feet guided her over worn linoleum riddled with unavoidable squeaks. Memories called to her from the quiet house. Her unfaltering steps took her to the room that had been her bedroom. Halting for just a moment, she was reminded of all the countless other times she'd walked over that very floor. And for that moment she felt as if this time was nothing more than a continuation of all those other times.

Standing in the middle of the room, her heart swelled with the blossoming feelings of belonging. Uncle Mick had left the room exactly as it had been seven years ago. She'd come back often those first years. After all, this was the only *real* home she knew. But, except for the brief stay three weeks ago when Uncle Mick had first suffered his stroke and hurried snatches of time at holidays, she hadn't really been home in two years.

This time, arriving home was different. Uncle Mick wasn't sitting in his old recliner listening to the weather report for the Great Lake. He wasn't walking Old Red along the village outskirts. Instead, Uncle Mick lay in a hospital room, learning to regain the use of the left side of his body. Old Red had grown slow and tired. He now lay in his final resting place beneath the soft grass at the foot of a huge lilac bush in the backyard. The house was quiet and lonely without them.

And a stranger, a man by the name of Shane Wells, was nearby, churning the deep waters of her sense of security. For a moment Starr felt like the ten-year-old girl she'd been; an orphan, adjusting to the loss of her parents, coming to live with a man old enough to be her grandfather.

But that sinking orphan feeling didn't remain. A smile tugged at her memory, buoying her spirits.

Uncle Mick. In the Great Lake of childhood, he had been her lifeboat. Mick Mahoney hadn't known exactly what one did with a ten-year-old child. And she hadn't known quite what to make of the red-haired Irishman, the last descendant of a deceased lighthouse keeper, who had opened his home to her. However, it was so natural, as if it were meant to be, the way the two of them became a family.

Only now another man threatened to steal her family from her.

Trying to clear her mind of those thoughts, she took off her robe and slipped her nightgown over her head, staring into the mirror as the soft, midnight blue material conformed to her body.

She remembered the way Shane had watched her from across the restaurant. His look had been steady and sensuous. Another flash of loneliness stabbed at her. It was the same kind of loneliness she'd seen deep in his eyes. She stood there, blank and shaken, in the bedroom she'd cherished as a child. Shane hadn't come here loud and demanding. Instead he'd come silently, searching for his own answers.

I hope he finds proof that Uncle Mick isn't really his grandfather. Let there be proof!

Starr turned away from her own reflection, feeling selfish and guilty. She wanted to dislike him. She wanted to hate him. And she'd never hated another living soul in her entire life. But she couldn't hate him, couldn't even dislike him entirely. For some reason she felt a transparent bond between them. Loneliness.

Why did her thoughts keep returning to that man? Before she'd even known his identity, he'd drawn her thoughts. Before she knew his name, he'd had an alluring, intriguing, secretive quality. But she'd assumed she'd never see him again.

She'd encountered Shane three times so far, and each meeting had caught her completely off guard. Starr wrapped her warm chenille robe securely around her, then padded into the kitchen where she opened the refrigerator, automatically searching for bottled water. After a moment of staring at the nearly empty shelves, she remembered that people here didn't buy bottled water. She closed the door, reached for a glass, and turned on the tap.

These past two days were only the beginning. She knew she and Shane would meet again. The size of this town alone would make it inevitable. But there was another reason to see him again. The only reason that mattered.

Uncle Mick.

When Starr had finished drinking the cool tap water, she left the glass on the counter and stared into the blackness beyond the window. The darkness blinded her, as blind as she was about what the future might hold. Of one thing she was certain; the next time she saw Shane Wells, she'd be prepared. Her future depended on it.

Out of habit, she locked the door, then crawled into bed. For a long time she listened to the faint night sounds of home. She'd forgotten how *quiet* it was here. Not a horn blared nor a siren wailed. Only the wind whispered in the trees. The stillness soothed her as nothing else could.

What were the chances that Shane really was Mick's grandson? There had to be a logical explanation. Shane couldn't have much to go on, or he wouldn't be here digging for answers. Tomorrow she'd find out what he knew.

As her eyelids grew heavy, she smiled into the darkness. What really mattered was that Uncle Mick was going to be all right. This business with Shane was probably all a big mix-up.

Just before falling asleep, she thought, *Tomorrow I'll stock the pantry and refrigerator. I'll buy fruit and vegetables . . . and . . .* Her eyes drifted shut and sleep came.

The next thing she knew sunlight slanted across the bed and spilled over onto the worn carpet. Starr was sprawled on her stomach across the entire bed, the blankets pulled out, the sheet a jumbled mess at her waist. She pushed her tangled hair from her eyes, then squinted against the sunshine to see the bedside clock. *Nine o'clock!*

She'd been more exhausted than she'd realized. Starr threw back the blankets and sprang to her feet. She had a lot to do. And she didn't appreciate beginning her day behind schedule.

"Shane?"

From his position, flat on his back beneath his car, he turned his head to the right where Starr's voice had come from. All he could see were her legs, from feet to knees. Narrow black boots, laced to the ankles, were planted a comfortable distance apart. Jade green socks peeked over the tops. His gaze traveled over the few inches of bare leg between her socks and the lace-tipped edges of skintight black leggings.

With little effort Shane shimmied out from under the car. In one lithe movement, he was on his feet, not even bothering to brush the dust and gravel from the seat of his jeans.

"Yes?" The word broke on an audible breath. Shane swore to himself. Had it really been *that* long since he'd seen a woman in tight pants that he couldn't even fake his way through idle conversation? What ever happened to topics like the weather?

"I went to see Uncle Mick last night."

"How is he?"

"Getting stronger. But that isn't what I came to tell you."

In her behalf, he had to admit that her long, jade-colored shirt wasn't tight fitting and did cover her from neck to hips. And it wasn't her fault the April breeze plastered the fabric to her body, outlining the shape of her breasts, conforming to the curve of her hips.

But then, it wasn't his fault either. He couldn't remember a time when he'd had such trouble with the fit of his jeans. He envied the wind for its ability to press itself to her soft curves. *Think of something else, dammit.*

Her next statement cut into his thoughts. "We need to talk. About Uncle Mick."

Her words affected him like a cold shower. He took his time wiping his oily hands on the cloth hanging from his front pocket, squared his shoulders, then met her gaze.

She'd fastened her hair at her nape with a shiny clip. Her face, devoid of makeup, was pale, her skin flawless. But it was her eyes that captivated him. She looked up at him with large hazel eyes framed by a sweeping of light brown lashes.

Shane sucked in a quick breath. *She looked vulner-*

able, dammit. Vulnerable and something else. He waited for her to continue, half in anticipation, half in dread.

"Uncle Mick asked me to find the truth. And just for the record, I'm going to try to prove he isn't your grandfather."

Saucy. Vulnerable and saucy. And tart. What a combination. The cold shower effect hadn't lasted long. "I see. Well, just so we understand each other, I'm going to try to prove that he is."

"And how do you intend to do that?"

Shane settled his hands on his hips and took a deep breath. Instead of meeting her eyes, he looked into the distance, toward the lighthouse over a mile and a half away. He willed the tightness below his waist to go away.

With an underlying sadness, he replied, "I'd intended to ask your uncle about that summer."

When she started to protest, he interrupted her. "I'm not totally insensitive, Starr. I know he's not up to it. I won't ask him now."

"All right. I'm not totally insensitive either. Why don't you begin by telling me what you know? Ask Uncle Mick about *what* summer?"

Why did she want to know about that long-ago summer? She'd made it perfectly clear she didn't appreciate his digging into the past. He searched her face for malice. Not a shred was evident. His instincts told him to trust her. But he didn't trust his instincts anymore. They'd failed him with Jazz. Jazz had paid for the mistake with his life.

"Why do you want to know?" When her gaze flew to his, Shane immediately regretted his harsh tone.

"Look, Shane, if you continue to answer my questions with more questions, we'll never find our answer."

It was the word "our" that tipped the scales in her favor. *Our answer*, she'd said. That one word did something to his heart. He only hoped it didn't affect his better judgment.

He searched for a way to tell Starr about his grandfather, about Jake's final conversation. No words would form. Without making a sound, Shane turned on his heel. In order for her to follow him inside, she'd have to partially trust him. If she did, he'd try to explain. If she turned and left, he'd continue his search alone.

Shane stood inside the cabin, with his back to the door, listening. Nothing. He didn't hear a sound, not footsteps on the step, not the creak of the doorknob. A painful knot tightened in his gut. A permanent sorrow seemed to weigh him down.

A car in dire need of a new muffler rumbled by, brake torquing in the loose gravel. *Starr must have left.* Shane reached for his scribbled notes of Jake's final words. With the pages grasped tightly in his fist, he turned.

Starr watched him from across the room. The change in his posture from one moment to the next made it clear he hadn't heard her come inside. His gaze was now fixed on her, his brows drawn down, forming two creases between his eyes.

For a moment she saw hurt and longing glint across his irises. The look was replaced by a sudden expression of disbelief. Starr searched for a plausible explanation. *He didn't believe I'd follow him. He thinks I don't trust him.*

Something stirred within her heart. Did she trust him? She walked farther into the room, noting the sturdy furniture and old flooring, the cheap prints hanging on outdated paneling. "Nice place."

Grooves lined each side of his mouth, the left deeper than the right. Starr was pretty sure laughter hadn't put them there. The creases between his eyes disappeared and one side of his mouth moved the tiniest bit. "Thanks. You like cottage chintzy, too?"

For a moment she held her breath. He'd almost smiled. "Uncle Mick does."

He didn't seem to know what to say to that. Instead of pursuing idle conversation, he looked at the wrinkled papers in his hand. Starr shortened the distance separating them. Her gesture an entreaty, she reached her hand toward him. For the first time since she'd seen him, Shane's movements were stiff, as if he were reluctant to part with an important legacy.

He loosened his grip slowly, allowing her to take the papers from him. "You probably won't be able to read my handwriting."

"I'm a nurse. Believe me, your handwriting couldn't be worse than some of the doctors' I deal with." As she studied the chicken scratches across the page in her hand, she reconsidered.

As Starr carefully deciphered the words on the first page, a lump formed in her throat. These were words of love, a man's memories of a woman named Hannah and a little girl named Kate.

"Is this man your grandfather?"

"Was. Turns out he wasn't. Not really."

"You're sure?" she asked.

"He said so. That's all the proof *I* need."

It was obvious Shane had trusted the man. His tone dared her to contradict that trust.

"He died?" she asked quietly.

Shane nodded. "Two hours after telling me all this." He pointed to the words filling the pages in her hand.

She read on. Whoever this man was, he'd known Mick. And he described the lighthouse perfectly. His words were haunting. A cold shiver ran up Starr's spine. *So maybe he'd vacationed here years ago. That didn't mean Mick had fathered a child.*

"Was he coherent? I'm a nurse, Shane. I've seen patients who are facing death babble about nothing."

"He was there, Starr. His mind was sharp, right to the end."

She read the words on the last page. *It never mattered, Shane. Kate was my little girl. And you're the son I never had.*

Tears gathered behind Starr's eyes. On the day Starr had left for college, Uncle Mick had uttered similar words to her. "I know it's scary leavin' home for the first time," he'd said. "Just remember, ever since you were a wee lass, you've been the daughter I never had. You'll be a fine nurse." As if the sudden burst of emotion had made him uncomfortable, Mick had squatted down to scratch behind Old Red's ears.

Starr swallowed the lump in her throat at the memory. "Where are your parents, Shane?"

"They both died. A long time ago."

"Was Kate your mother?"

"Yes."

If Kate really had been Mick's child, then Starr wasn't the "daughter he'd never had." He'd *had* a daughter, a real daughter. The possibility shook her sense of security.

For a long moment Starr looked into Shane's eyes. Unblinking, his dark eyes became still. His look was intense, his cause clear. It reminded her how Uncle Mick had looked when he'd asked her to find the answers.

"Are you with me? Or against me?" His voice dropped. So did his gaze.

"I promised Uncle Mick I'd find the truth. And since that's all either of us is seeking, I guess I'm with you."

She handed the jumbled notes to Shane. "These are wonderful mementoes. They must mean a great deal to you." She touched a fingertip to a fine gold chain concealed beneath her shirt. "But that's all they are. Mementoes. I'd put them in a safe place if I were you because they're very valuable. But we both know they're not evidence. They prove nothing. Where did you plan to begin?"

His expression didn't change throughout her speech. And she thought he must have been very good at whatever it was he'd done in Chicago.

"I'm going to start with county records. I've been through all Jake's things. And my parents'. As far as I can tell, my mother was born in a hospital in this county."

"Then that's where we'll begin." She turned and strode from the cabin. Taking a deep breath she waited for Shane to follow. If he did, there would be no turning back.

Shane strode past her without a sound. He peered at his car's engine, tightened something or other, then closed the hood with a sharp *clank*. "You can get in. I have to wash my hands and lock the doors."

Starr opened the passenger door, then watched him walk toward the cabin, becoming accustomed to the way he moved, as quiet and sure as the wind. Before he reached the wooden stoop, she called, "You don't have to do that here, you know."

Upon reaching the top step he turned. "Do what?"

"Lock your doors. Uncle Mick says locks only keep out honest people anyway."

Without reply, he disappeared inside. Minutes later, he climbed behind the steering wheel. Starr wondered if he'd turned the lock on the cabin door.

Shane leaned close and she held her breath. Rather than commenting on her reaction to his nearness, he tucked an envelope into the glove compartment and said, "Mick sounds like a wise man." His voice was so low, it stirred something inside her. He gunned the engine, the tires spinning in reverse. She pushed away the warm feeling and clicked her seat belt firmly in place.

"So, what did you do in Chicago?" she asked.

"What do you think I did?"

Did he ever simply answer a question? "Drove a race car?" she inquired.

The groove at the side of his mouth deepened. His lips lifted and his face relaxed. She grasped the armrest as he sped around a corner.

"Hardly. I was a police officer."

She had a feeling he was a lot more than that. "Will you go back to it?"

"I don't know. Will you go back to nursing in New York?"

"I don't know."

They were at it again, Starr thought. Asking questions without answers. She directed him to the next town where the county courthouse was located. He parked his car, then took the envelope from the glove compartment. Together they walked up the steps of the old building.

After pausing to catch her breath Starr began to speak. "A young doctor was supposedly the first white man to settle in this area. He treated the Indians and fur traders. This place didn't exactly catch on. Because of the Great Lakes, Michigan was inaccessible on three sides. The settlers who did brave the elements had hard lives. They drained the swamps and swatted the mosquitoes."

Shane remained silent. Her voice stole over him like a song. When it didn't look as if she was going to continue, he coaxed her with a question. "What else?"

"Well, it's been reported that two years before they began the construction of this courthouse a fur trader shot and killed a bear right about where we're standing now."

"I didn't know there were bears around here." He hoped she'd continue. Come what may, he could have gone on listening to the sound of her voice forever. That she'd share this piece of folklore touched him. He felt an eagerness to touch her in return, both physically and emotionally. And Shane seldom touched anyone.

"Well, there aren't many, not anymore. Bears still live in the Upper Peninsula, though. They'd have to travel the five miles along the Mackinaw Bridge to get to the Lower Peninsula."

They'd reached the county clerk's office. Shane

suddenly felt nervous. He didn't know what he'd find. He only prayed his answers were close at hand.

"Can I help you two?" a woman asked. "Are you here to get a marriage license?"

Starr and Shane gasped together.

Shane stepped to the counter. "I'm interested in obtaining a copy of a birth certificate."

"Yours?"

"No, my mother's."

"Is she living? Because if she's living, we can't give you that information without her written consent."

"No, she's deceased," he said automatically.

"I see," the woman answered skeptically. "In that case, I'll need to see proof that you're a family member and that she is indeed deceased."

Shane swore under his breath. These county agencies were as bad here as everywhere. Red tape. Nothing but red tape. He took a copy of his mother's death certificate from the envelope. After the woman read it carefully, he handed her a copy of his own birth certificate, identifying the person who had died as his mother.

The woman folded the copies, then slid them back into the envelope. She looked up at Shane, obviously wary of the tall, brooding man.

Starr sidled up next to him. "Is everything in order?" she asked the other woman. Her tone hinted at friendliness. Her voice said *trust me*. As a nurse she probably had cranky patients wrapped around her little finger in no time. Out on the streets, she'd have crooks eating out of her hands.

"Well, yes," the woman replied.

"Great. How do we go about searching for his mother's birth certificate?" Starr asked.

"Genealogy research is open between eight and one Tuesdays and Wednesdays. Follow me. I'll show you where to begin."

Shane followed behind Starr. He took in the old green paint on the walls, the high ceilings, the ancient light fixtures. They traipsed through mazelike corridors until they reached a small room with a noisy radiator and no windows. The old, slightly musty room was as quiet as a country church. Shane looked at the shelves of thick books; books filled with names of people who were born in this county, others filled with names of people who had died here.

"These books are dated, the certificates entered in chronological order." The woman looked from Starr to Shane.

"Thank you," Starr whispered. "You've been extremely helpful. If we have any questions, may we drag you from your work again to help us?"

Shane watched Starr with growing fascination. She'd effectively dismissed the other woman without offending her, extracting a promise of help in the process. "How did you do that?"

"Do what?" Large hazel eyes innocently searched his.

"You had that woman in the palm of your hand."

"Patience opens more doors than irritation. And patience keeps them open," she stated.

"Another of Mick's sayings?"

"Hardly," she quipped. "This one's my own."

She threw his equilibrium off kilter. Shane blamed it on those huge gray eyes. Not to mention the way her hips swayed in those skintight pants. But it was more than that. When she walked past him, the scent of roses mingled with the smell of musty books. She affected his breathing, not to mention his thought processes. She'd used her patience tactics on that other woman. He wondered if she was using them on him.

"Let me see those certificates, Shane." She rested her hand on his arm.

He looked into her upturned eyes. Heartrending worry darkened them to a deep gray. Why was she so afraid of what they might discover? She hadn't lifted her hand, and Shane had a sudden impulse to pull her into his arms. He wanted to protect her from whatever hurt she feared.

Before he could openly respond, she moved away. As he watched her reach for a book more than eight inches thick, he decided it was probably just as well she'd put a little space between them. The skin where she'd touched him felt warm long after she'd lifted her hand away.

In a low voice, Shane told Starr the date of his mother's birth.

"She'd be forty-nine years old," Starr replied.

Shane didn't answer. He sometimes had trouble remembering his mother. And he couldn't imagine her at forty-nine.

Starr leaned over a low table and began to leaf through the old pages. "My mother would be forty-five. She was a flower child. I wonder what she'd be like today."

"A forty-five-year-old flower child?" he asked.

Starr smiled, but didn't look up. As she continued to turn the old pages, a fine gold chain swung from the neckline of her shirt. Two charms dangled from a heart-shaped link.

Shane took the charms in his fingers, the delicate

chain a tremulous connection to Starr. He leaned closer, inspecting the two tarnished peace signs. One spelled the word "peace" with curving letters, the other a circle containing a "V," the symbol for peace.

Starr held her breath. He was so close, she could smell the pine scent of his aftershave. When his gaze met hers, she nearly drowned in the mysterious depth in his eyes. She felt a fluttering in her heart, saw an infinite understanding in his look. He'd lost both his parents, too. He knew what it was like to be orphaned.

Only she had Uncle Mick. And he had no one. Or did he?

"Your parents' own legacy?" His voice was heart-poundingly deep. Her gaze dropped to his mouth, to the grooves at either corner of his lips. She wanted to press a soft kiss to those lines, to wipe away, if only for a moment, the aloneness that surrounded him.

The sound of ringing telephones from the next room permeated their reverie. Shane carefully replaced the necklace inside her shirt. His touch was completely platonic, yet she felt an odd sense of intimacy at the gentle brush of his fingertips along her neck.

She forced her attention to the records book. As she neared the proper year, her progress slowed. Shane held each page as she skimmed it. Starr avoided contact, visual or otherwise. The atmosphere in the tiny room grew more ominous with every turned page. *Could it really be so simple? Could one old document actually be all the proof Shane needed to take her place in Mick's life?*

"That's it!" His words cut into her contemplation. She skimmed the document. Shane did the same. Her heartbeat pounded in her ears. Shane's breathing was rapid.

Kathleen Elaine Brockmyre, daughter of Hannah L. (Lewis) Brockmyre and Jake H. Brockmyre.

Starr breathed a sigh of relief. The document clearly listed this Jake as Kathleen's father. Jake. Not Uncle Mick. But even as she felt relief course through her, she also felt Shane's sadness, his disappointment.

He pulled the book from her grasp. Leaning closer, he inspected the old-fashioned writing. "It looks like something was erased in the father's name space. I wonder why they erased the first printing?"

Starr gazed into Shane's eyes before leaning closer to the document for a better look. "You can't be certain anything's been erased. Jake's name is printed clearly. Accept it, Shane."

"Jake told me the truth, Starr. That's what I'll accept. Nothing less than the truth."

Shane closed the book, then replaced it on the proper shelf. He looked around the room one last time. Dead ends. That's all he'd found from the moment he'd started searching. "Let's go."

He watched Starr straighten her spine and square her shoulders. But she didn't utter a sound. She was angry because he hadn't accepted the document as proof. There had to be another way to prove that Mick Mahoney was indeed his grandfather.

On their way out the door, the woman who'd

helped them asked, "Did you find what you were looking for?"

"Yes," Starr answered.

"No," Shane replied at the same time.

Neither said another word until they'd driven several blocks. Starr broke the brooding silence. "You're not going to give up until you find the answer *you* want, are you?"

"I'll stop when I find the truth, Starr. That document wasn't our answer. It simply raised more questions."

Starr didn't answer. She didn't trust her voice. Or her tongue. She should have known he wouldn't take the word of a certified, legal document. She should have known.

FIVE

Starr didn't utter another word as Shane sped around corners, burning out his frustration, increasing her own. Neither did he. Until he came to a screeching halt at the curb in front of Mick's house.

"Are you still with me, Starr?" The revving engine punctuated the question.

She turned in her seat. Looking him square in the face, she tried to imagine how she'd feel if the tables were turned, if Uncle Mick's name had been printed on that document. The lines between his eyes were back, the grooves at the sides of his mouth more prominent than ever. He looked tired-soul weary. His disappointment was too raw to discuss, so he'd closed her out. A heavy ache dropped to her chest.

She released a long, slow sigh, wishing there were a way to absorb some of his disappointment. But she didn't know what to say, didn't know what to do. She should have felt like dancing for joy. Instead she felt sad.

"Looks like we're between the proverbial rock and hard place, Shane. But I guess I'm still with you."

As if unused to reaching out, his fingers encircled her hand, then stilled. Her gaze traveled over his face and searched his eyes. For a moment he studied her intently. Then the lines between his eyes disappeared and the grooves at his mouth diminished. His touch on her wrist was whisper soft, the look in his eyes masculine warm.

He leaned closer, so that she held her breath, anticipating his next move. She watched his eyes close, heard him take a deep breath, as if he were fighting to remain aloof.

There was one way she could soothe him, reach him, if only for a moment. Starr leaned closer, faintly brushing her lips over his. She touched him, as sweet and soft as the gentle breeze. With that one touch, she wanted him to know, for this moment, he wasn't completely alone.

It was Shane who broke the kiss. Pulling slightly away, he opened his eyes. The look she saw there made her yearn for something unattainable. Mingling with surprise was a look of warmth, and she knew he'd accepted the kindness she'd offered. Then his large hands cupped her face. Before she could breathe, his mouth covered hers, his lips firm and warm. Her lashes swept to her cheeks, her heart dove to her stomach.

His fingers toyed with the hair clasp at her nape. A heartbeat later it fell to the seat with a faint *clink*. His lips lifted from hers and his fingers splayed through the chaotic strands of her hair. Then his mouth found hers a second time. With this kiss he gave something to her, something warm, something unique.

The kiss broke slowly. She opened her eyes to find him watching her. His look started melting a part of her that had been frozen deep inside. Starr gave him a tremulous smile before grazing the line at the left side of his mouth. With slow deliberateness and a brush of her lips, she moved to the other side. As she eased the grim line away, her lips a soothing caress, a sound escaped from somewhere deep inside him, possibly from his very soul. The sound, like hurt giving way to pleasure, drew her lashes down, filling her with new longing.

Shane pulled her into his embrace, covering her mouth with his own. His kiss drew feelings from her until Starr no longer knew who was doing the giving. And who the receiving.

He moved his mouth over hers, the warmth of his lips melting her senses. Their lips clung, their breaths mingled. Her limbs became lethargic, her being filled with languidness. Never had she felt such temptation to forget about the rest of her life, to simply explore the moment.

Before her better judgment melted completely away, she slowly ended the kiss. Taking a deep breath, she didn't quite meet his eyes, her gaze fixed on his mouth instead.

That kiss had snowballed into so much more than she'd intended. It would take analyzing to understand how it had happened. For now, she simply wanted to change the subject. "What will you do next?"

His lips stretched and he raised one eyebrow at her loaded question. "Next?"

Color tinted her cheeks. But it had been worth her

discomfort to see his half smile. She pulled a face at him, rolling her eyes and clicking her tongue. "I mean about Jake's final words."

"I don't know." His answer was noncommittal, as if he were reluctant to open a barely healed wound. He smoothed her hair away from her face with surprising gentleness before he continued. "But I'll find the truth. Some way, I'll find it."

Her own smile evaporated. He'd search for *his truth*, no matter what it did to her. Starr jerked on the door handle. Without turning back to Shane, she said, "Jake described the lighthouse perfectly. He must have spent some time there. Maybe Hannah did, too. That's the next place to look."

"Are you coming with me, Starr?"

Longing deepened his voice. Starr tried not to hear. "I promised Uncle Mick I'd come to the hospital to see him this afternoon. I'll bring you the key when I'm through."

"We both know I don't need a key to get in."

Her earlier words about locks only keeping out the honest people hung between them. "I know. But I'm going with you. And we'll use my key."

The patch of rubber he laid pulling away didn't surprise her in the least. Shane Wells was a stubborn man. A stubborn man on a mission.

An hour later Starr paced from one end of the small hospital room to the other as she waited for Uncle Mick to come back from physical therapy. Her thoughts were still churning, her stomach tied up in knots. She'd thought kissing Shane would alleviate his loneliness. Instead it had accentuated her own. It wasn't something she planned to do again.

The truth, Shane had said. He'd stop at nothing less than the truth. And Starr knew there wasn't a thing she could say to change his mind. He had Jake's word. She knew better than to question it. She fidgeted with the chain around her neck. What she needed right now was to talk to Uncle Mick. She needed his reassuring presence.

When he reentered the hospital room five minutes later, she was relieved.

"It didn't go well, aye, lass?"

There was no sense wondering how he knew. The door swished shut behind her as she tried to form a reply. Mick Mahoney settled himself more comfortably in the high-backed hospital chair. "You wouldn't be munching on a candy bar, now, unless somethin' or someone's upset ya."

"How was your therapy today?" She effectively changed the subject.

"It went fine." His look told her the subject of Shane Wells could wait. But not forever. "It isn't my fault that old battle-ax of a nurse doesn't see things my way."

Starr smiled. Uncle Mick's presence was working its magic on her nerves. "Exactly what doesn't she see your way?"

"Those walkers are horrible contraptions. I'll walk out of this place with a cane."

"But Uncle Mick, what if you fall?"

"Walkers are for babes. Or old folks."

Although he didn't look or act his age, Mick was seventy-one years old. Starr wondered if he'd ever admit to being old. She also knew if he didn't *want* to use a walker, there was no use arguing with him about it.

"She called me a stubborn old fool." He snorted. "I'm a far cry from being old." He didn't dispute the *stubborn* portion. "And I was only a fool once."

"When was that?" With a serious expression, she watched him.

"A long time ago, lass. A long, long time ago."

She waited for him to continue. But Mick had said all he intended to say on the subject. He was stubborn, all right.

As stubborn as Shane.

Starr left the hospital an hour later. Uncle Mick had asked her about Shane Wells. She'd described what they'd found in the county records, told him of Jake's dying words, how he'd described the lighthouse. She watched for Mick's reaction. He'd simply nodded. There was something Uncle Mick wasn't telling her. And it sent a cold shiver all the way to her toes. That shiver stayed with her as she drove home. She felt cold. Cold and hungry. Her stomach growled, reminding her she'd completely missed lunch.

After sliding the large old lighthouse key from its peg behind the kitchen door she took a quick look inside the refrigerator. There was little to eat here.

She drained a glass of cool tap water, then hurried back out to her car. Eating would wait. For some reason, giving Shane the lighthouse key would not.

Five minutes later she stood on the wooden step, knocking on Shane's door until her fist hurt. *I hurried, for heaven's sake. And he isn't even home. His car is parked in the driveway. Where can he be?* Her stomach let out another low rumble. Starr looked around her one more time, wondering if he'd gone on to the lighthouse without her. If he had, there was no sense hurrying to give him the key. He'd picked the lock to get inside the first time she'd met him. She didn't doubt he could do it again.

When her stomach growled again, she pushed her hair from her face, then climbed back inside her car. A few minutes later she'd parked along the street in front of the grocery store. She pushed the cart around the narrow aisles, stopping to chat with other shoppers along the way, carefully choosing staple items and canned goods from the old shelves. She ran into Joanna, quite literally, at the fruit and vegetable stand near the back of the store.

"This is just like old times, isn't it?" Jo asked gaily. "I love it when you're in town, Starr."

"So do I. But why are you in such a good mood?" Pregnancy had made Joanna even more beautiful. Yesterday she'd seemed tired of the whole thing. Today she looked happy.

She grinned as she patted her stomach. "This condition only seems like it's going to last forever. I've just come from Dr. Shepiro's. He told me the baby could come any day."

Just then Maybell appeared, stacking more fruits and vegetables on the crowded stands. "Tut, tut, tut. Three weeks from yesterday, that's when *that* baby will be born." She pointed the bunch of carrots in her hand at Joanna's midsection. "The moon will be full, then. That's when *she'll* be born."

"She?" Starr mouthed to Jo.

"Full moon?" Jo mumbled under her breath. "I'm having a baby, not a werewolf."

"I heard that," Maybell admonished. "Three weeks from yesterday. Mark my words. And your calendar.'' She hurried away, her white head bobbing above the top of the shelves in the next aisle.

Joanna shook her head. And Starr began to laugh. It was a small sound at first, but as Joanna continued to talk about werewolves and backaches and tongue-wagging know-it-alls, that gentle chuckle grew into ripples of deep, genuine laughter.

Starr finished choosing her groceries. As she pushed the cart up the last aisle she noticed several shoppers had surrounded a display of brightly colored towels. "Leave it to May to put a display of towels in a grocery store," one woman declared.

"But don't you just love these colors?" another responded.

Starr didn't look at the other shoppers. She remembered the threadbare towel she'd used the previous night and automatically reached for a pair of bright pink towels. When the towels didn't budge, her gaze flew to the person holding them firmly from the opposite side of the display.

Shane's eyes bore directly into hers. She stared wordlessly at him, her heartbeat thudding in her ears. Starr felt him release the towels but her eyes didn't leave his. He tipped his chin, then gave her a half smile. After he'd placed another towel in his basket, he strode toward the cashier.

She watched him go. It reminded her of the second time she'd seen him—in this very store.

Chocolate. That's what she'd forgotten.

She pushed her cart past the shoppers still raving about the towel display. Maybell was ringing up Shane's purchases, keeping up a steady stream of conversation all the while. Starr looked up as she passed the counter. Maybell and Shane both turned their eyes to her.

She looked from one to the other, only to find Maybell shrewdly doing the same. Starr cut around a corner, sputtering to herself. *That's all I need . . . Maybell's nose for gossip.*

She was still sputtering and her stomach was still growling a half hour later as she put away the last grocery item and closed the cabinet door. Now when she opened the refrigerator, the shelves were filled with edibles; colorful fruits and vegetables and meat and eggs and cheese . . . and chocolate.

A hard fist rattled the kitchen door. Starr spun around to find Shane peering through the glass. Hurrying to the door, she turned the lock. She counted to five and took a deep breath before opening the door to Shane.

"I thought you said you didn't lock your doors here."

As far as greetings went, she'd heard friendlier ones. "I didn't say that. I said you didn't have to."

He stood in the doorway, silently watching her. She looked back at him, unblinking, unsure what to say. She watched his eyes travel over her, from her hair to her toes. His look made her aware of her wind-tousled curls and her form-fitting clothes. Her outfit had fit right in in New York. This very definitely was not New York.

Then his gaze left her and swept over the old-fashioned kitchen, as if by taking in the black-and-white tiled floor and old-fashioned cabinets, he might come to know its owner. As if reading his mind, she said, "Mick is a lot like this kitchen, Shane. Old, yet sturdy. Clean and proud. Useful and full of life."

They stood an arm's length apart, he in the doorway, she still grasping the knob. And Starr realized that it would always come back to this. No matter how his look drew her nearer, no matter how his kisses had melted her, Uncle Mick lay between them.

In that moment of thick silence, her stomach growled hungrily.

"Have you eaten?" he asked.

She shook her head.

"I was on my way to the Main Street Café for dinner. Want to come along?"

"Did you find anything at the lighthouse?" she asked.

"The lighthouse?"

"You haven't been to the lighthouse?"

"Why would you think I'd been to the lighthouse?" Shane grumbled. "Don't you trust my word?"

Starr realized they were at it again; answering questions with more questions. "I stopped by your place earlier. You weren't home. Have you been to the lighthouse today, Shane?"

"You stopped by my place?"

"Just answer my question. Have you?"

She didn't move, didn't even blink as she waited for him to answer. He lowered his voice, being purposefully mysterious. "I've been a lot of places this afternoon, Starr. But your lighthouse isn't one of them."

She sucked in a quick breath as his lips lifted into a smile. The sound of his voice affected her deeply, but not as deeply as his little smiles.

"So, will you?"

This time she raised her brows at him. "Will I what?"

"Have dinner with me?"

She released the breath she'd been holding. Swinging the door open wide, she said, "Would you like to come in, Shane? It'll just take me a few minutes to freshen up."

For the first time in his life, Shane walked into Mick Mahoney's kitchen, into the home of the man he believed was his grandfather. His heart rate didn't quicken, his breathing didn't become irregular. Nothing changed. Until Starr turned.

"I'll just be a minute." She tossed her words over her shoulder along with her wild hair. With a delightful sway of her hips, she disappeared through another door. She hadn't answered his question about dinner with words. But he was becoming accustomed to another form of communication. Her eyes told him things he'd never heard before. And that little sway of her hips had his own body responding in a way that made words completely unnecessary.

They'd missed the usual supper crowd. As Starr and Shane munched on juicy burgers and thick wedges of fries, they found themselves alone in the restaurant. Something about him was different. She couldn't put her finger on what it was, but something between them had changed. It was a kind of awareness, a mutual attraction, a link.

Maybell had stopped by their table, an inquiring glint in her eyes. Starr introduced Shane, then breathed a sigh of relief as he held his head high and met May's look and her strategically placed questions, literally charming her to the roots of her curly white hair without giving her a drop of fuel for gossip.

When Maybell had gone, he turned his gaze to Starr. His looks were more rugged than handsome, yet she'd never been so aware of another man's inherent strength and sensuality. He held his head high like a man used to being alone, unbeaten by that isolation.

"People would pay you a fortune to teach them how to do that," she murmured.

"Do what?"

"You turned away May's questions with so much subtlety she won't realize you were hedging until next week."

"A trick of the trade."

"The police trade, Shane? What type of police work were you in before coming here? And don't try hedging. I'm onto you."

He'd known she'd ask sooner or later. But the subject of his occupation was a sore one. The reason for his leave of absence lay buried in a Chicago cemetery. Jazz. That kid had gotten to him from the beginning. His life had stretched Shane's capacity for understanding. His death had shaken Shane's belief in himself.

"I was an undercover police officer in Chicago."

No wonder he had the look of a devilish hero, of a man who'd seen too much.

"Was?" she asked.

"Yes." That was all he said. She imposed an iron will on herself to keep from asking for more. Starr had thought there was some link between them. She now realized that was impossible. Shane had no one in his life, didn't even have a job to go back to. He could dig up Mick's past, search for his connection to the Mahoney bloodline. He had so much to gain from such a search. He'd gain a grandfather, a home, a new life.

She was the one who would lose.

"Did you want to order dessert?" His deep voice broke into her troubled thoughts.

"No." She pushed her chair back, then stood. Reaching into her purse for Dottie's tip, her fingers brushed the cool metal of the lighthouse key. She'd promised Mick she'd find the truth about Shane. In order to fulfill her promise, she'd have to continue to search. She was left with an inexplicable feeling of emptiness.

Starr stalked out of the Main Street Café without turning, without looking back. But she didn't doubt, not for a second, that Shane was right behind her.

They were both silent as they got in her car and headed west out of town, toward Lake Michigan and the lighthouse. She veered to the right at the fork in the road, bouncing over the rutted path. Upon reaching the lighthouse property, she pulled around to the far side, near the cottage entrance.

"I understand what you meant by safe driving."

She tried to conquer her involuntary reaction to his attempt at dry humor. And lost. A smile tipped her full lips. "Let that be a lesson to you. Safe and sure. That's my motto." Starr took the key from her purse. "Now for lesson number two." She inserted the key, dramatically turning it in the lock.

An amused look came into his eyes. "Too easy." Shane pushed through the heavy cottage door. A sudden change came over him. He tensed beside her. Starr looked up at his stern profile and fear prickled along her spine. His eyes were squinted, the telltale lines in his face more pronounced than she'd ever seen them.

"What is it?" For some reason she found herself whispering.

Shane didn't answer her. His gaze traveled over every inch of the cottage's interior, silently categorizing each dust-covered piece of furniture, every nook and corner.

He didn't speak until he was satisfied that nothing was amiss. "This door creaks and groans like a ghost in an attic." The hair on the back of her neck stood up. She imagined him in a dark alley, face to face with the long shadows of wanted criminals, and shivered in the twilight.

"Of course it creaks. It's seldom used."

"Then why have the hinges on the lighthouse door, the one facing the lake, been oiled?"

"I don't know." Her answer only raised more questions.

"Does anyone else have access to the lighthouse?" he asked, slowly turning around, viewing the interior with a practiced eye.

"Not with the key. Not that the lack of a key kept you out," she reminded him.

He roamed about the cottage, opening drawers, peering into corners, shining his flashlight up the chimney. She tiptoed, stopping directly behind him. "What are you looking for?"

Shane jumped, then swore under his breath.

Starr smiled in spite of herself.

"I don't know. But something's here. I felt it before. And I feel it now."

"Something? What?" She held her breath as he shone his flashlight about the cottage.

He heard the fear in her voice. She was afraid of what he might find. He was afraid of what he might never find. Their goals were oil and water, a crazy mixture of fear and hope. No matter how often they mixed them, they'd never remain united.

The fading gray light shining through the windows grew more dim with every passing minute. "It's no use," he grumbled. "We won't find anything else tonight. It's getting too dark."

She slowly took in the cottage's interior. "When I first came to live with Uncle Mick, I used to imagine that I'd live here when I grew up. I'd sit in the tower for hours dreaming about the people who used to live here, the lighthouse keepers and their families."

Her voice worked over him like magic. If their goals were really totally opposite, why did her voice reach inside him like a gentle balm, restoring a tiny portion of his belief in the future? Shane didn't want to go back to his rented cabin. Alone. He wanted Starr to keep talking—for a few minutes, for a few hours, forever.

He was becoming accustomed to the tight fit of his jeans, to the knot that thudded in his gut, and lower. Since meeting Starr he'd felt alive again. For the first time in a long time, he was glad that he was.

They left the cottage. While Starr locked the door, Shane looked skyward. Darkness had fallen over the Great Lake. And stars were beginning to twinkle in the cloudless sky. The moon was a curved hook on the horizon. He had a vague memory of his mother's mellow voice soothing him to sleep after his father's death. She'd believed in wishes made upon stars. So had he.

Shane watched Starr stroll toward her car. He wished he believed in them now. "Are you in a hurry to get home, Starr?"

She turned toward him. "Not really."

"Then let's take a walk."

She led the way, past her car, between the trunks of tall pine trees, to a narrow path. They walked on in silence until they came to a bend in the trail. A hundred yards farther the trail opened into a large clearing.

Darkness lay all around them, the faint illumination from the moon and stars casting only enough light for them to make out the nearby shoreline and clumps of trees behind them. The breeze blowing off the Great Lake felt cool against his skin.

Starr must have felt the cold breeze too, because a moment later he heard a rasp as she closed her jacket zipper to her neck.

"We can go back if you're cold, Starr."

"No. Not yet. I haven't been out here in the dark in years."

"Tell me about this old lighthouse and its keepers." He watched her turn her head toward the lighthouse, invisible through the trees. After a moment, she began, her voice blending with the waves, the darkness, and the breeze.

"This lighthouse was built by the Federal Lighthouse Service a hundred years ago. Uncle Mick's grandfather was its first keeper, his father its second. They came from Ireland. And in the isolation here, they maintained their strong Irish heritage. Mick's father married a young Scottish woman visiting this area. They took over the upkeep of the property. To this day Uncle Mick's speech is a unique mixture of Irish brogue and Scottish lilt.''

He marveled at the smile in her voice. "How did Mick come to own the property?"

"The U.S. Coast Guard became responsible for lighthouses in 1939. They built a taller, more powerful structure five miles north of here. This light was no longer needed. It was just Mick and his father by then. When the property came up for sale, his father purchased it."

"And you dreamed of living here when you grew up.''

"Silly, little girl dreams.''

She obviously believed in dreams come true as much as he believed in wishes upon stars. If he did believe in wishes, he'd wish to hold her in his arms. His wishes wouldn't stop there.

Layers of pine needles muted his footsteps, yet Starr knew the exact moment he stepped closer. His fingers brushed her hand, then gently took it in his.

"You're cold. We should be getting back.'' His voice was deep and whisper smooth. It drew her like temptation. She slipped her fingers between each of his. Then, slowly, side by side, they began to pick their way along the trail.

When they reached the bend, she murmured, "No matter how this turns out, Shane, if you want to hear tales of winter storms and shipwrecks, Uncle Mick is the person you should talk to.''

She heard his deep breathing, felt his hesitation a moment before he turned her to him. She couldn't make out his expression in the darkness, just the outline of his head and shoulders. His last kiss lingered around the edges of her memory. And Starr felt it again, a wavering connection to this stranger.

"You chose nursing as your career. An extremely giving, draining occupation. And you came back here to help Mick recover. You greet everyone in this town with a smile. It's obvious everyone here loves you. But tell me, Starr, does anyone ever give anything back to you?"

Her heart seemed to swell within the confines of her ribs. She knew Uncle Mick loved her, yet he wasn't really *her* uncle. She called this her home, but it wasn't really *her* hometown. Her birth certificate wasn't on file in the county courthouse. She'd been born on a commune in northern California.

As she looked into the shadows on Shane's face, she understood why his search was so important to him. His search had nothing to do with money. It had to do with belonging. In that respect, they were the same.

His hand found her cheek, and she leaned into its warmth. For once in her life, maybe only for this moment, she'd found a kindred spirit. She knew she could reach out to him in this darkness, ignore who he was, ignore who she wasn't. For this single moment in time, she wanted to trust in their shared longings, luxuriate in their mutual attraction with no need for explanations.

Just for this one moment in her life, she could reach out to someone. She could reach out to Shane. For the second time that day, this time for an entirely different reason, Starr leaned closer. Standing on tiptoe, she raised her mouth to his.

SIX

In the darkness, touch took the place of sight. Her hands slid up his arms. His palm held her face. The evening wind cooled her back, while Shane's nearness warmed the rest of her. She closed her eyes against the night, tipping her chin up, ever closer to his.

His warm breath tingled against her lips a moment before their mouths touched, retreated, then met again. Her warm, moist lips clung to the fullness of his. Her body softened as his grew taut. They each met the kiss halfway, as if this joining were separate from their search, a kind of neutral territory.

Touch and smell. In the darkness she was filled with those senses. He was warmth and smooth leather, scented of pine and fresh air. The late-night stubble on his cheek tickled her palm, his nearness massaging her with silver moonbeams.

Starr turned her head, his lips trailing up her cheek, resting at her temple. She breathed deeply through her mouth, too emotion filled to speak. No words were necessary.

Shane spread his fingers through her hair, bringing her face up for another kiss. All the air seeped out of her lungs on a gentle sigh. She slid her hands across his shoulders, stretching her body over his.

He released a deep breath. His arms encircled her back, pulling her hard against him. Starr was entranced by his silent strength.

"Starr." His deep voice rasped over her name like the wind echoing down a chimney, sultry, swirling, sensuous. The sound filled her ears, blending with the sounds of the waves on Lake Michigan and the breeze whispering through the pines. Or was that the sound of her blood rushing through her veins?

Without warning, Shane straightened. And withdrew.

Starr's head swam at the sudden change in him. He placed a finger to her lips. The muscles in his shoulders that had been pliant a moment ago suddenly went rigid.

After a moment, he whispered, "Stay here."

"What is it?"

"I heard something. I'll be right back." He turned and with silent footsteps headed for the lighthouse. Starr was no more than two steps behind.

He stopped so abruptly she ran right into him. He swore under his breath. "I told you to stay."

"I'm coming with you."

The trail was swallowed up by towering pines, the faint starlight unable to filter through their widespread boughs. With her heart beating in her ears, Starr picked her way through the darkness.

They stopped. Concealed within the shadows of

the trees, Starr breathed deeply. Her gaze swept across the view, taking in the lighthouse, cottage, and shoreline beyond. She saw nothing.

Tension radiated from Shane. He was poised, listening, watching. Ready. Just then a movement caught her eye. Two shadows crept from the lighthouse, through the unrevealing darkness, toward the shore. For long moments only the sound of waves lapped the shore. Then one engine sputtered to life in the distance, followed by another, both disappearing into the night.

"Why did they row so far before using their engines?" she asked.

His answer barely cut the silence. "For the same reason someone oiled the hinges on the lighthouse door. To minimize the chances of detection."

"But why?"

"I don't know. But you can bet there's a reason." After several interminable minutes, Shane declared, "I'm going to have a look. Stay here until I'm sure it's safe."

"I'm coming with you."

"Dammit, Starr. I won't argue with you."

"Good. Let's go."

He clamped her wrist in his grip. "I mean it."

"So do I." They faced each other, their wills silently battling like a Mexican standoff.

He tried another tack. "You could get hurt."

His concern for her safety touched her. But she wasn't backing down. "There's safety in numbers."

Shane relented. He realized he had no choice. Unless he bound and gagged her, she was coming with him. *Stubborn woman.*

They crept to the side of the lighthouse, then circled around to the back, the pine needles cushioning their steps, muting their progress. Shane surveyed the entire area before moving out into the open. He was aware of Starr's breathing, could practically feel her heart hammering in her chest. Just as he'd felt it flutter wildly when he'd kissed her.

The woman had gotten to him. She touched him with her smiles, moved him with her kisses, infuriated him with her stubbornness. She distracted him. Plain and simple.

He couldn't afford to be distracted by romantic notions. He'd come here, to this town, alone. He expected to leave the same way. A familiar pain gripped his heart.

So far he'd come across nothing but snags in his search for his ancestry. Now his search had led him to something else. He inspected the lighthouse door. It was locked up tight. But he knew from experience the simple lock wasn't difficult to pick.

Something was going on here. Something secretive. And his line of work had taught him one thing; people who used darkness as a cloak were seldom on the right side of the law. If he wasn't careful, Starr could get tangled up in whatever was going on here. Her life could be in danger. She was just stubborn enough not to care. Jazz hadn't cared. Shane refused to let Starr end up with such a fate.

In the light of day, Shane crouched down at eye level with the lock. It took only a moment to spring it open. He replaced the pointed metal object in his pocket, then pulled on the knob. Once again the heavy old door swung open on silent hinges.

Sunlight slanted through the opening. Fresh footprints were etched in the dust. Shane measured the print with his own shoe. This print had been made by a tall man, a man with feet the same size as his own.

He surveyed the structure. Nothing had been changed. Questions strummed through his mind. Who would break into the lighthouse in the dark? And why? Not teenagers intent on ransacking an old building. Nothing had been touched. No graffiti adorned the walls, no windows had been broken.

He closed the door, then stalked about the small area. After a moment he took the stairs, turning at each landing until he'd reached the top. Shane strode directly to the windows. Gazing into the distance, his mind was a tangled mixture of Jake's final words, this new turn of events, and Starr's kisses.

Shane's car was parked at the end of the lane, directly beneath the weathered No Trespassing sign. In the lighthouse was exactly where she'd expected to find him. She pulled the door open, then let it close with a loud bang. "Shane?" She hurried up the stairs.

The look in his eyes stopped her at the top. Starr took a deep breath, winded from her fast climb. She raised her chin and boldly met his gaze.

"Are you crazy? Why not broadcast the fact that you're a woman, alone, in the middle of nowhere? How did you know I wasn't an intruder, a thief, or a murderer?"

She remembered thinking that very thing the first time she'd met his eyes here in this tower. "I saw your car."

"Starr, I want you to stay away from here."

"Tough." She watched his mouth clamp shut in surprise. The lines in his face were back. He didn't look like anyone she'd care to meet in a dark alley. "Have you found any clues?"

"No. Nothing. I mean it, Starr. From now on, I search alone."

"That's what you think."

He'd shut her out, as if he'd wiped her from his memory. She only wished she could forget his kisses so easily.

"Until I know who's using this place, and why, I want you to stay away from here." His tone made it clear he didn't intend to listen to any argument.

"Jake spent time here. Maybe Hannah did, too. I promised Uncle Mick I'd find the truth. I keep my promises, Shane." Her vow weighed upon her. Shane's attitude added to the heavy ache.

He gave her a narrow glance. "I don't want to have to worry about you."

She didn't answer him. Instead, she turned and slowly descended the stairs. He didn't want to have to worry about her. She didn't especially relish the idea of worrying about him, either. But she had no choice.

Starr picked her way over stones and pebbles toward the shore. The wind lifted her hair and swirled it across her face. She pushed it behind her ears, aware that Shane stood watching from the tower. She folded her arms in front of her, then looked out across the Great Lake. Today thin clouds streaked the horizon. The deep water of Lake Michigan was a dark blue gray.

Michi-guma, the Indians living on these shores had called it. Big water. Indian words were simple, full of meaning. White Cloud, Running Deer. Big Water. She wondered what they'd have called Shane. Her thoughts churned as deep and dark as the lake. The hand at her shoulder made her nearly jump out of her skin. She sprang around. "Shane! You scared me half to death."

His eyes looked deep into hers.

Silent Eagle. That's what the Indians would have called Shane Wells. He was a big man, yet he moved without a sound. And the silence behind his eyes spoke of things he'd never say.

She pulled her gaze from his to the gentle slope of land from shore to the lighthouse. Sunlight glinted off a shiny object lying on the rocks. Starr hurried to investigate. Leaning down, she picked up a pair of old spectacles, the frames tarnished with age, yet the glass lenses still intact.

Shane took the glasses from her, turning them over in his hand, deep in thought. "This is strange," she murmured. She watched his expression, then added, "These couldn't have washed this far up the shore."

"No."

When he didn't continue, she thought out loud. "So, someone had to drop them. These are old, older than both our ages put together. I've seen spectacles like these someplace." Her mind filled with trying to remember. "At the Great Lakes Shipwreck Museum at Whitefish Point."

"In a museum?" he asked.

"Yes. Why would someone drop these antiques here?"

"I don't know, Starr. But I'm leaving first thing in the morning. And I want you to stay away from the lighthouse."

"You're leaving?" Her eyes clung to his, only to find him analyzing her reaction.

"Promise me you won't come here until I get back."

So he wasn't leaving for good. She couldn't even begin to understand the wide spectrum her emotions skittered through. Surprise that he was leaving. Uncertainty. Relief that he was coming back. More uncertainty.

"Promise me, Starr?"

"Do you trust my word, Shane?"

She thought she might drown in his look. The wind in the trees and the waves lapping the shore faded. Gazing into his eyes, the fragile bond between them seemed to grow stronger. She'd promised Uncle Mick she'd find the truth. Starr suddenly felt ill equipped to undertake such a task. Still, she waited for Shane's reply.

When it came, it was weighted, thoughtful. "Your word means a great deal to me."

"Then I won't come back here until you return."

He released a deep breath. She hadn't been aware he was holding it. Sliding his hand inside his jacket pocket, he turned and strode toward the lighthouse.

Starr ran to catch up. "Where are you going, anyway? And how long did I just promise to stay away from this place?" She watched his face, silhouetted against the sunshine. One side of his mouth twitched. "Careful, Shane. You almost smiled."

When he'd reached his car, he turned to face her. Satisfaction pursed his mouth. His mellow baritone was edged with something rich, like caramel. "You've amazed me since the first moment we met."

"Yeah? Well, you're pretty amazing yourself. Are you trying to avoid my question?" she asked.

Laughter floated up from his throat—rusty, sincere. The sound did crazy things to her emotions. He brought his hand from his pocket. With his other hand he reached for hers. She watched him open his fist, revealing the clasp she'd worn in her hair the day before. The clasp that had fallen to the seat, forgotten, when they'd kissed.

He placed the barrette in her palm, then wrapped his fingers around hers. "I have to testify at a hearing in Chicago. I should be back in a week." He looked from her face to the lighthouse, then back again. Just before climbing into his car, he added, "Remember Starr, I have your word."

Starr didn't reiterate. She pressed the smooth barrette into her palm. The clasp felt warm in her hand, warmed by his. She inclined her head in a slight nod. And smiled.

The following morning Starr opened her eyes to darkness. For the first time in as long as she could remember, she felt she didn't *have* to hurry out of bed. Her thoughts were as lazy as her mood. She thought of Uncle Mick, of his steady smile, his cantankerous nature. She muddled through the possibilities concerning the strangers in the lighthouse. And she thought of Shane.

She gained no insights from her thoughts. But she didn't mind. She wasn't looking for insights. There would be plenty of time for those later. She had an entire week to do nothing but think.

By the time she awoke in the early morning hours of her third day, she'd had all the introspections she could stand. She'd kept her word and hadn't ventured anywhere near the lighthouse. She'd visited Mick twice each day, answered his questions, and listened to his views. She'd overheard Maybell's gossip and confided the reason for Shane's visit to Joanna, who was still counting the days. Starr told herself she didn't have her own reason for counting the days. She knew she was lying.

On the morning of her fourth day she wrapped herself in her warm robe, then tiptoed out to the kitchen, over the squeaks and creaks of the floor, to start a pot of coffee. Uncle Mick was the only person she knew who still made coffee the old-fashioned way, in a percolator on the stove.

When the coffee was brewed she took Uncle Mick's big mug from a peg and filled it with fresh hot coffee. She padded into the living room where she sank into Mick's favorite chair. Light spread onto the carpet in the elongated shape of the kitchen doorway. She turned her back on the room and sat facing the window, sipping and thinking, as light slowly seeped into the April sky.

Uncle Mick's gold pocket watch lay on the table. She picked it up, following the smooth surface with the pads of her fingertips. She snapped it open, watching the second hand sweep around the numbers, counting *one-Mississippi, two-Mississippi, three-Mississippi* to herself.

She sat alone in Mick's chair, drinking from his mug. Yet it was Shane she missed. She wondered if it were possible to miss someone you didn't love. She hoped it was and prayed she didn't.

Starr jumped to her feet. She had to find something

to do. Waiting had never been something she'd done well.

"Ah." She luxuriated in the warm bubbles swirling around her, completely relaxed. She smoothed a sponge over her shoulders, then down each arm. Next she hummed, her soft brush keeping time to the music blaring from the radio on the floor as she scrubbed paint specs from her fingernails.

For the past three days she'd worked until her muscles ached. But it was a good kind of ache, the ache of accomplishment. Mick's kitchen, living room, and bedroom shone with coats of fresh paint. She'd turned on the radio, tuned out her worries, and painted. Starr had a feeling that no matter how this turned out, no matter who was Shane's true grandfather, no matter who was using the lighthouse, she'd have plenty of time to worry. Later.

The bubbles slid down her bare skin like a caress. She tugged at the plug's chain with her toe, then pressed her face into the fluffy new towel. With the terry towel wrapped securely around her, Starr flipped the radio off.

And froze.

The water draining from the bathtub formed a mini-whirlpool. But that wasn't what she'd heard. With one hand grasping the doorknob, the other at the delicate chain at her throat, she listened. Her thundering heart was all she heard.

Another *creak* from the kitchen floor put her mind in a state of panic. She knew the exact location of that particular creak. Starr searched the tiny bathroom for a weapon. After flipping off the light, she grasped the wooden handle of the plunger and silently turned the doorknob.

The door squeaked the tiniest bit. Starr cringed at the noise. On tiptoe she zigged and zagged around the creaks in the hall floor.

Holding the towel up with one hand, she burst around the corner. "Hi-ya!" she screeched, waving the plunger like an ominous threat.

Shane didn't bother to swear under his breath. He ground out a whole slew of expletives, none of them mild, at incredibly loud decibels. "HI-YA? Where in the hell have you been?"

She opened her mouth to speak.

"I knocked until my knuckles bled. Lights are on all over the house. All I could think was that you went to the lighthouse and some thug followed you home and did God only knows what to you."

She again tried to explain. But he wasn't finished with his tirade. "I sweat blood and you come out wearing a towel and waving a plunger and shouting hi-ya!"

Her shock evaporated and her dignity kicked in. "Don't you yell at me, Shane Wells. *I* didn't just break into this house. *You* sweat blood? Well, mister, you're not the only one."

Her hair was escaping the loose knot on her head at an alarming rate. Starr realized she was still pointing the plunger at Shane like a sword. She lowered it to the floor, then leaned it against the newly painted wall.

With every ounce of dignity she could muster, she clutched the towel with one hand and reached for her hair with the other. She slowly worked the hair loose, untwisting and smoothing it, until she felt the tendrils cascade down her back in a waterfall of curls.

Shane's heart changed tempo. It didn't slow down, exactly. His blood had rushed through his body like freight trains when she hadn't answered his knocks. Fear had driven him then. Something else drove him now. His first instinct upon finding her safe was to throttle her. His second was to rip that towel from her body and kiss her senseless.

In his thirty years of life, he'd experienced a myriad of emotions, but he'd never experienced desire in quite this way, as if something deep inside him was awakening, coming alive. The atmosphere practically crackled between them. He took one giant step toward her. She seemed rooted to the spot, her eyes never leaving his face, waiting. He didn't even try to disguise his body's reaction.

Her face looked smooth as satin in the soft light, her neck and shoulders proud. Her hair framed her face and shoulders like a mist. Shane reached for a lock that had strayed to the front of her shoulder, he, a man who seldom reached toward anyone. The waving tendrils felt incredibly soft as he combed them back with his fingers.

His fingertips followed the delicate chain at her neck. "Do you ever take these charms off?"

"Never." Her voice was no more than a whisper. That one small sound changed the tempo of the blood pumping through his veins yet again.

"You wouldn't believe the thoughts that barreled through me when you didn't answer your door." His fingers followed the chain to the back of her neck, where they spread through her thick hair.

"I gave you my word I wouldn't go near the lighthouse until you returned," she whispered.

"But a week is a long time."

"Six days."

So, she'd counted them, too.

Her hair was so incredibly soft, her eyes the gray blue of the lake. He smoothed his thumb over her cheek. She turned her face toward his touch.

The scent of roses hovered over her skin. Shane knew a sudden need—time to explore with this woman, time to give pleasure, time to receive. He was aware of what she was wearing, of what she wasn't wearing. He took another step closer. The floor squeaked beneath his feet.

The sound seemed to remind Starr of where they were, of who they were. She laid her palm to his cheek, then retreated. "Shane, I'm standing in the middle of Mick's kitchen wearing a towel." She took a step back.

"I know." His eyes took on a devilish glint. "Believe me, Starr, I'm totally aware of that."

Goose bumps suddenly rose along her flesh, not only from the cold. "I'll be right back." This time she didn't even try to avoid the creaks in the floor. She just hurried to her room where she let her towel slide from her body. She wrapped her long robe around her, then tied the sash securely at her waist.

She glanced at her reflection in the tall mirror. Satisfied that she was covered from head to foot, she took a deep breath, and waited. She heard the first squeak, then the second and the third. In the mirror, her eyes met his.

She'd never seen such a dreamy look in any man's eyes. The lines in his face were completely gone.

His lips were parted slightly. Such kissable lips. He leaned against the door frame, more at ease than she'd ever seen him. His gaze left hers, then traveled over the old-fashioned dresser, the white ruffled spread, the shelves of dolls and games.

Her gaze followed his. This was clearly a child's room. Not a woman's room, a room where a woman could take a lover. She knew it. And his look told her he did, too.

"Is there someplace we could go to get a cup of coffee?"

She walked toward him. "How about the kitchen?" For reasons she didn't want to explore, she didn't want to break this tremulous connection between them.

He brushed his palm over the satiny material of a deep blue nightgown draped over a chair near the door. Starr wet her lips, mesmerized, as if that gown covered her body, as if his fingers warmed the skin underneath.

"How was Chicago?" Her voice sounded quivery even to her own ears.

"The same. How's Mick?"

"Better. He's coming home next week." Starr had thought Uncle Mick was the biggest force keeping her and Shane apart. Now she realized she may have been wrong. There was something else, something Shane had left in Chicago. Or something he'd lost there. She stepped over the damp pink towel on the floor. "Now, for that coffee."

She watched him take in the appearance of her room, from her damp towel on the floor to the hair clasp lying on the dresser to her clothes hanging over chairs. "Not exactly a neatnik, are you?"

"I know where everything is. Besides, a person

who breaks and enters shouldn't call another person names."

"I didn't break and enter, exactly." It was his first attempt at humor.

It wasn't lost on Starr. "No, you picked and entered. As far as I know, Shane, this is the first time in this town's history someone's broken into a home here."

"As far as I know, this is the first time in history, period, someone's been attacked by a lady wearing a red towel, flailing a plunger, and screaming Hi-ya!"

Color tinted her cheeks as she realized how she must have looked. Trying to regain a portion of her dignity, she marched past him on her way to the kitchen. "I was provoked."

"I see," he murmured, following her.

"They taught that hi-ya! maneuver in a self-defense class I took when I first moved to New York. This is the first time I've used it." Starr knew she was talking nonsense to keep from thinking about the way Shane made her feel. She reached for two oversized captains' mugs, sugar, and cream.

"And the pink towel and plunger?"

"I improvised." She stopped pouring to look at him. The expression on his face sent mixed feelings surging through her. He seemed to be fighting their attraction with as much might as she. The look in his eyes had her wondering which side would win. It also reminded her of cravings.

She tore her gaze from his, stalked to the refrigerator, and extracted two large candy bars. In unison, they tore off the shiny wrappers and bit into chocolate and caramel. It wasn't exactly the same craving they'd ignited earlier. But it was the only one that would be appeased that night.

SEVEN

From across the room Shane stopped sweeping, leaned on his broom, and watched Starr. They'd been searching for an hour. All they'd stirred up so far was dust.

Even though her hair was tucked into a loose braid, the tendrils seemed to defy order as much as she did. She left doors ajar, drawers open, and furniture askew as she searched. She was wearing the same faded yellow tee shirt she'd worn the first time he'd seen her. The Say Yes to Michigan logo stretched over her breasts exactly as he remembered. She'd affected him then. She affected him now.

She rocked back on her heels and swiped her hands along her dusty jeans, evidently oblivious of his unwavering gaze. A knot formed in his stomach, a knot of desire, and something else. She sneezed, a high *ah-chooo* sound, then straightened. Opening the door of a tall cabinet, she stretched on tiptoe as she peered inside. Finding nothing, she dropped back to her heels, then placed one hand to the small of her back, rotating her shoulders.

The knot in his gut swooped lower. Shane tore his gaze from her, then made another swipe at the floor with the broom. *I'm supposed to be searching for clues about my ancestry and all I can think about is the way Starr looked in that towel last night.*

When Starr sneezed again, the broom handle clattered to the floor. She turned just in time to see Shane disappear out the door. Hurrying to the doorway, she called to his back. "Is something wrong?"

He turned. Squinting against the high-noon sun, he met her look, then let his gaze trail away. "I'm going to wait for the dust to settle." With that, he strode toward the water's edge.

She donned her red jacket, then ran to catch up. Keeping her distance, she picked her way over the rocks and pebbles near shore. He was quiet. Even quieter than usual. *Uncommunicative is more like it.* For a man who had everything to gain from this search, he didn't seem very interested in finding his answers. He'd been pensive since returning from Chicago.

"What did you find out about those old spectacles we found?" she asked.

He shoved his hands into his pockets and began to follow the shoreline. Starr did the same.

"Shane?"

He turned with a start, as if her question had pulled his thoughts from someplace far away. "One of the guys in the department owed me a favor so I had him check them out. They *are* old, over seventy years old, in fact. And from the corrosion on the frames, he said they'd been in the water for a long, long time."

"I wonder why they suddenly turned up on our shore."

"I doubt they just *turned up*. Someone had to have dropped them there." On the next breath he asked, "How long has Mick owned the lighthouse?"

"It's been in his family for over fifty years. Why?"

"No one's ever broken into it before?"

"Besides you?" At his serious look, Starr shook her head, murmuring, "I don't think so."

Shane stopped walking to stare back at the lighthouse. She perched on the edge of an overturned rowboat several yards from the water's edge. After loosening her shoe, she tipped it upside down, dumping a small pebble onto the ground.

Gazing at his back, so ramrod straight, she remembered how it had felt beneath her palms. What little wind there was ruffled through his soft hair; Starr remembered its texture beneath her fingertips. Once again she wondered about his silence, wondered about his pain, wondered if she was falling in love with this stranger.

"Shane." She watched his gaze swing from the lighthouse to her. He met her look with a closed expression. She looked deeper, searching for a sign of what he was thinking, of what he was feeling. She couldn't tell from his expression.

"Whose boat is that?" he asked.

"Uncle Mick's. But he hasn't used it in years."

"Let's take it out." He dropped to his knees, running his palms over the smooth wood. For the first time that day, he seemed animated, excited, alive. She hated to spoil this sudden change in him. But take a boat on Lake Michigan?

Starr looked out at the waves on the lake, at the old rowboat, then back again. "Now?"

He was already turning it over, tugging it toward the water. "This old thing weighs a ton." He strained against its weight. "Come on, Starr, let's have some fun."

Fun? She pushed with all her might, wondering if she had enough nerve to actually ride in it.

A moment later Shane broke into her reverie. "Hop in. I can manage the rest of the way." He tossed two heavy old oars inside, then waited for her to comply.

She climbed in, immediately gripping the sides for dear life. Shane heaved the boat into the water. In a lithe movement he gave it one last shove and jumped in as a wave caught them up, pulling them out into the deeper water.

He must be a devil. Only a devil could make me agree to a ride on Lake Michigan. Shane immediately began to row. And Starr searched the entire floor within her scope of vision for holes.

"Relax." A male voice cut through her panic. It took her a moment to realize that voice belonged to Shane. Her gaze rose to his. "Starr, what is it?" He continued to work the oars, his muscles straining against the waves. But his gaze didn't stray from hers. His eyes burned into hers, compelling, deep. She clung to his look as to a buoy in a raging storm.

Then his look changed. And she knew he cared, truly cared, for her, about her. She looked away, out toward the sun glinting off the small waves. "My parents drowned in this lake."

"I'll take you back to shore." That simply, he'd accepted her fear. Without question. Without explanation.

She forced her fingers to loosen their grip on the side of the boat. "No."

"You're sure?"

She laughed a shaky laugh. "For now. Just don't go far from shore."

"I promise."

She met his look. And she knew she could trust him. He continued to row and she watched his muscles strain, taut and strong. "Guess I'm just a chicken at heart."

"I'd call you several things. But chicken isn't one of them."

"Well, it's true. Ever since my parents drowned, I've been afraid of the water. I read somewhere that personality traits are genetic. But neither of my parents was afraid of the water. My chickenness must have been a recessive gene."

"That theory is as leaky as this old boat."

Her gaze darted about the floor at his mention of a leak.

"There's no leak, Starr. Just a play on words." At her sigh of relief, he asked, "What were your parents like?"

She looked at her white knuckles, then into Shane's eyes. "They were unusual. No other little girls had parents like mine." At his skeptical look, she added, "Honest. They were true flower children of the sixties. They believed in peace and tranquility and love."

"Honorable beliefs." Most people laughed or rolled their eyes when Starr told them that. Not Shane. It made her yearn to know him, really know him; what he was like as a child, what he wanted for his future. He seldom answered questions about himself. She wondered if he'd ever open up to her. "What were *your* parents like?"

He turned the small boat toward shore before answering. "They weren't hippies. But their beliefs were similar to your parents'. I have only vague memories of them. Jake raised me for the most part and I always looked for a similarity to him. Now I understand why I never found one. He said I'm like Mick."

His look challenged her to deny Jake's final words. Starr didn't even try. It always came back to this. When she felt on the verge of knowing him, of loving him, it always came back to Mick.

The boat scraped bottom. The sound grated on her nerves, like his words had grated on her hope that Shane was wrong about Uncle Mick.

He hopped out of the boat, hauling it farther up the shore. Starr carefully did the same. They both remained silent as she helped him pull it completely out of the water. While he tipped it upside down, she crossed her arms in front of her. With her back to Shane, she said, "In a sense, we're a lot alike, you and I. Both orphaned, both raised by wonderful old men. We both deal with death in our work and in our lives."

"Do you miss your work in New York?"

She hadn't expected his voice to be so close. "Not really. I want to make a difference. But I can do that anywhere."

"No ties?"

"To New York? Not really. Patients come and go. The special ones I remember. But my only real ties are here. What about you? Any ties?"

"No. There was a kid back in Chicago. But he's gone."

"He died?"

Shane nodded.

"Is he the reason you left Chicago?"

"He's the reason I went back." They'd started walking, slowly, not touching. "I was a key witness at his murderer's trial."

She shivered at the dangers he'd faced. "And was the murderer convicted?"

"Yes."

"How does that make you feel?"

"It won't bring Jazz back."

"Jazz?"

"He was a street kid, smart and tough. Barely fifteen. But he wanted out, out of that life, away from those streets. He almost made it. I did my best to see that he did. But it turns out my best just wasn't good enough."

He blamed himself for his young friend's death. Starr had never felt such a burning, intense desire to reach out to another human being the way she wanted to reach out to Shane. She wanted to touch his very soul. Instead she took his large hand in hers.

The gesture froze him to the spot. Undaunted, she took his other hand as well. "Shane, you made a difference in his life. That's more than he would have had without you. We can't save them all. I remember calling Uncle Mick after I'd stood help-lessly by while a patient slipped away. My first. He listened to my sobs, then told me only a power greater than I could save them all. He said the ones we lose keep us human."

Shane felt human, all right. Raw. He'd told her more in one afternoon than he'd told another human being, other than Jake, in his entire adult life. He'd opened himself to her and she'd absorbed his feeling of inadequacy concerning Jazz. Then, after all was said and done, she'd reached out to him, touched him. She'd taken both his hands in hers. And she'd touched him.

She gave. Without asking for anything in return, she gave to him. No one had done that. Not since he was a kid. Not even Jake had touched him quite the way this woman had.

He brought his hands, still in hers, to Starr's face. Her grip loosened; her fingers slid to his wrists. Her eyes seemed to cling to his. He brushed his lips along her forehead, her lashes sweeping his cheek as they fluttered closed. He inched his fingers to her temples, then gently followed the delicate curve of her ears before splaying wide into her loose braid. With utmost care, he lowered his mouth to hers. He kissed her with surprising gentleness, a gentleness he didn't know he was capable of expressing, a gentleness he didn't know he was capable of feeling.

She was warmth, velvet warmth—her hair, her skin, her lips, her heart. His own heart began to pump in overtime.

She sighed and Shane absorbed the sound the way she'd absorbed his feelings about Jazz. He deepened the kiss and felt her shudder, felt her soften in his arms. And Shane knew, if only for now, she accepted what he offered.

It took a moment for the low, menacing growls to penetrate. With lightning speed, he reacted. He ended the kiss and placed himself between Starr and those snarls all in one movement.

The growls instantly ceased. Shane stood looking

into the soulful eyes of a dog, a skinny, black scrap of a dog. A mutt.

"Look, Shane, a stray." Starr stepped around him. Leaning down, she crooned, "Aren't you a pretty little thing. Where's your folks?"

Pretty? She's got to be kidding. "Careful, Starr. She could be wild, rabid."

Starr was kneeling over the animal. "I doubt it. Hungry is more like it. Come on, Shane, let's run back to the cottage and find her something to eat."

A few minutes later she rummaged through the picnic basket in the trunk of her car. She tore a corner from her egg salad sandwich and offered it to the dog. In one gulp, it disappeared, followed by another, and another, until the entire sandwich was gone.

"Oh, Shane, she's still hungry. Do you mind if I give her yours, too?"

He wondered what they'd eat for lunch if the dog devoured theirs. "Be my guest." Next he watched as she poured iced tea into a cup, then held it for the dog to drink. He'd never seen anyone pamper an animal more in his life. And this particular animal had interrupted his kiss.

"Now that you're satisfied, can I have a look?"

Her voice had been syrupy sweet and Shane raised his eyebrow in Starr's direction. But she'd been speaking to the dog. She scratched behind the animal's ears and patted her head. "She's wearing a collar, but no tags. That's strange. Do you think she's lost?"

"Dumped is more like it."

She stared into the dog's black eyes. Those eyes had seen a lot of pain. Her coat looked worn. She was skinny. And her eyes were older than time. They reminded her of Shane's eyes. "I'll put an ad in the newspaper. But for now, I think I'll call her Trixie. Unless you want her, Shane. I mean, you did see her first."

"No, no. She isn't mine to keep or give away." Starr was on her knees near the dog. His voice drew her gaze up, up, until she found herself staring into his unfathomable brown eyes. "It isn't a question of who saw her first. She's attached herself to you. She's yours." As if that was all he intended to say, he clamped his mouth shut and strode back into the cottage.

Starr did *not* understand him. His moods broke faster than the waves on the lake. She held the cottage door for Trixie, then let it clank shut behind them.

Shane had resumed the task of sweeping. Bending down, he pushed the dirt into an old metal dustpan. Without speaking, he strode past her through the door, where he flung the dust into the wind.

She took an old linen tablecloth from the basket, then spread it across the table. Trixie had eaten their sandwiches, but they still had big, red apples and wedges of Colby cheese and plenty of iced tea, and, of course, two medium-sized candy bars for dessert.

When Shane strode back in, she watched him lean his broom against a far wall. "Hungry?" she asked.

He walked toward her. And once again Starr was struck by the way he moved. He was a big man, yet he moved like the wind. Big men shook the ground when they walked. They rattled dishes, moved furniture. Not Shane. Shane moved her. Big men were gruff. Rough. He could be those things. He was also gentle. And silent.

While they munched on cheese and apples and sipped iced tea, they talked. She told him about the lonely life of a lighthouse keeper before automobiles and telephones and televisions. "They battled the elements and their isolation. Each night they climbed the stairs and lit the light. In the old days they used oil. Of course, the modern-day lighthouses are fully automated."

"Modern technology." He took a bite of his apple. "What about this one? Does its light still work?"

"I imagine. Even though it's no longer used to warn ships in stormy weather, my uncle kept the lamp in working order. I think it always reminded him of his father and grandfather, of the old days when this old lighthouse was important, needed.

"Uncle Mick has a poem hanging in his bedroom about an old lighthouse tender replaced by an automated device. The author asks who'll polish the brass, who will, 'a cry for help in the darkness hear?' " Starr's gaze roamed about the cottage, imagining what life must have been like for the people who used to live here years ago when the lighthouse was in use. She thought about the isolation, the loneliness. She understood about loneliness.

She took a bite of her candy bar, then meandered to the stone fireplace, being careful not to disturb Trixie, who'd stretched out in a patch of sunshine. With the tips of her fingers she followed the outline of every stone. "In the movies they always find hidden documents behind a loosened fireplace brick."

"Anything can happen in the movies." He began

to search through an old desk against an adjacent wall.

When she was satisfied the stones all fit tight, she strode back to the table. Something teetered the tiniest bit beneath her foot. She went down to her knees, and pressed along the corner of the square tile. It definitely moved beneath her fingers. She cleaned the dust from its edges and bent closer for a better look. The tile wasn't fastened down.

Starr realized a shiver of panic. She was afraid of finding positive proof that Shane was Mick's grandson. Yet she knew she'd come too far to turn back now.

"Shane!" The note of panic in her voice brought Trixie's head up. It brought Shane bounding to her side.

"What is it?"

"This tile's loose."

He reached into his pocket. With a small pointed strip of metal, he pried up the corner of the tile. With little difficulty, he lifted the tile away.

Starr looked at the shallow opening in the floor. "A secret compartment." She pulled an old tin from the small space.

It took Shane a fair amount of prying to loosen the rusted lid. When it finally gave way, he handed the tin back to Starr. Her emotions whirled when she met his look. But she took the tin from his outstretched hands. She felt inside, where her fingertips brushed over a smooth leather surface. Carefully, she pulled a small book from the tin.

"It's a diary. And it's locked." She felt inside the tin for the key but found none.

Once again Shane used his pointed strip of metal, expertly delving the lock until the old mechanism grudgingly clicked open. And once again he handed the diary back to Starr.

She knew how important this search was to Shane. And she wondered what it had cost him to allow her first inspection. With a shaking voice, she read the name sprawled in flowing letters on the inside cover. "Hannah Louise Lewis. Shane, your grandmother's diary."

She held the cover for him to see. He nodded but pushed it back to her. "You read it, Starr."

She skimmed the first entry. And before her eyes, a young woman began to come to life.

April 28, 1942

Spring came early here in Shelby, Indiana. But Mother's winter-long battle with pneumonia has left her weakened. So father has decided to leave William in charge of the store and he, Mother, and I are heading north, to Pinesburg, a small village along Lake Michigan's eastern shore.

Tugging on her hand, Shane pulled Starr to her feet. "Your legs will get stiff if you stay like that. Let's walk. And you can read on."

Trixie followed close behind. Starr left her hand in his, a tiny gesture of trust that reached down into his heart. When they came to the trail through the pines, she opened the diary and began to read the second entry.

With her softly enunciated words she brought Hannah alive upon the screen of his imagination. Her voice was a gift, like a song, as much a gift as his grandmother's words, a grandmother he'd never known.

May 14, 1942
Lake Michigan is beautiful. There is water,
like an ocean, as far as the eye can see. And
trees, forests of them. I tore my dress during
my explorations today. So I bought a pair of
slacks. I didn't tell Father and Mother. They say
a woman who wants to be treated like a lady
should dress like one. Father grudgingly admits
that women working in the war industries sometimes need to wear them, but he says slacks will
forever alter the way men perceive womankind.
P.S. I should hope so!

Starr laughed at that. She couldn't imagine having
to hide the fact that she owned a pair of jeans. "Your
grandmother was ahead of her time." After she'd
read the first entry, she began to relax. And with
each entry after that, she became less worried that
this diary would disclose any new evidence. These
were simply the writings of a young girl on the
threshold of womanhood.

Starr read on. Hannah wrote of her new friends,
of her discoveries. When she mentioned the town
gossip named Maybell who worked in the general
store, Starr gasped. "Do you think she was May's
mother?"

"It's possible." Shane's voice was abrupt. It reminded her of what he was searching for, of how
important this search was to him. It started a shiver
along her spine.

She continued to read. Now, with each new entry,
her apprehension increased. Then her eyes scanned
a paragraph written on June 10, 1942.

I stood along the shore and watched as two young men rowed out to help a larger boat that had apparently run out of fuel. I'll never forget the way the sun glinted off one man's dark red hair. My heart seemed lodged in my throat as I watched their boat rock on the waves. I stood watch until they were both safely ashore. Jake Brockmyre and Mick Mahoney. Such a bantering pair, I've never before seen.

Starr didn't even realize she'd stopped walking. She was conscious only of a deep ache, a kind of hurt made up of fear and dread.

June 13, 1942
For some reason I am drawn, day after day, to the lighthouse. Both Jake and Mick are tall and handsome. Yet my eyes continually search for Mick. When he looks at me, I fear my knees will fail to support me. When I gaze into his deep brown eyes, I fear I will forget my own name. Others call me Hannah. But only Mick says "Lass."

Starr's voice trailed away. She couldn't go on. Her own knees had gone weak. Before her eyes, Hannah was falling in love with Uncle Mick. And if she'd loved him, she could have conceived his child.

She clamped the diary shut. "This isn't right. I shouldn't be reading this. It's private."

"It's the only way to learn the truth about that summer."

She flung the diary into his hand. "If she'd have wanted it read, Hannah wouldn't have hidden it."

"If she *hadn't* wanted it read, she would have burned it."

Why didn't she? Oh, why didn't she? "Then you read it. She was your grandmother." Starr crossed her arms in front of her chest and left Shane's side, stalking toward the cottage. Without turning, she knew he followed.

She felt a desperate need to see Uncle Mick. But what would she say to him? She knew she couldn't hide her emotions from his fatherly gaze. Cantankerous or not, he was as bright as an old sea dog.

The cottage door slammed shut behind her. Trixie whimpered on the other side of the closed door. Starr had forgotten all about the stray. She let the dog in, then began to gather up the remains of their lunch. Her candy bar lay on the table, barely touched. She felt no desire to finish it. This was one hurt chocolate couldn't soothe.

Instead of clearing the table one item at a time, she grasped each corner of the tablecloth, bringing everything together in one bundle, and stuffed it into the basket. She didn't care if Shane thought she had slovenly habits. She simply wanted to get out of there.

"Starr."

She grasped the basket in her hands before looking at him. With all her might, she tried to hide her inner misery from his probing gaze. "Let's go." She tried. But her eyes clung to the diary sticking out of his jacket pocket.

He took the basket from her hands and she locked the cottage door. Neither spoke again until they'd reached her car, where he said, "Maybe I should walk back to the cabin."

Her eyes met his over the top of the car. The

grooves in his face were back. She felt similar grooves in her heart. She held the seat forward for Trixie. "Don't be silly. I'm going right by your place." But she knew the sooner she dropped him off, the better she'd feel.

It didn't take her long to realize she'd been wrong. She didn't feel any better. Questions strummed through her mind. Questions about Mick and Hannah. And Shane.

The silence in her car during the short trip to his rented cabin had grown thick enough to slice. When she'd pulled into his driveway, he'd stared, hard, into her eyes. "I'll let you know what I find."

Without looking at him, without answering, she'd sped away.

He said he'd let me know. As she wandered from room to room, she strummed a fingernail up and down the delicate chain at her neck, producing a sound that resembled the buzzing of a lone mosquito searching for a midnight snack.

He'll let me know. I have to prepare myself for the possibility that Shane is Mick's grandson. But how? She paced from one room to the next. Her past and future became jumbled. Her thoughts were tangled. When the kitchen floor creaked beneath her feet, she paused, remembering the way it had creaked beneath Shane's step the previous night.

He'd almost kissed her, and she remembered how she'd held her breath. *You wanted him to,* her heart whispered.

Not so! her mind shouted back.

Starr paused in her pacing to catch her breath. Her fears were greater than ever. An hour had passed since she'd dropped Shane off. This pacing was doing her no good. It had left Trixie exhausted. She'd finally plopped to the floor where she watched her new mistress with soulful black eyes.

Starr needed to talk to someone. But she couldn't talk to Uncle Mick. He'd know something was wrong. And she wasn't ready to tell him what she feared.

Joanna. Starr hurried to the telephone, then jumped when it rang beneath her hand.

"Starr!" Joanna cried.

"Jo, I was just about to call you."

"My water broke." Joanna's voice was frantic. "David's in Traverse City. I can't reach him."

"How far apart are your pains?"

"Four minutes."

As a nurse, Starr knew second babies could come very fast. Her mind spun with worry but she laced her voice with calm. "Don't worry, Jo. I'll be right there."

Starr threw the receiver to its cradle, then turned with a jump when a hard fist rattled the door. Flinging the door open wide to Shane, she exclaimed, "It's Joanna. The baby's on the way and David's not there."

"I'll drive you," he stated. She hurried past him, realizing that with Shane behind the wheel, they'd arrive at Joanna's in record time. In her haste, she didn't turn off the lights or lock the door or say good-bye to Trixie.

She wished she hadn't noticed Shane lay the age-darkened leather of Hannah's diary on the kitchen table. But she *had* noticed, in spite of her haste, in spite of her fear. And Starr knew it was there. Waiting.

EIGHT

Pain etched Joanna's face. When she closed her eyes against another contraction Starr placed her hand along her friend's abdomen. "Concentrate on your breathing, Jo. I'm right here."

The tires spun in the gravel as Shane sped around another corner. Starr steadied herself and timed the length of the contraction, counting *one-Mississippi, two-Mississippi, three-Mississippi*, wishing she'd remembered to slip on her watch.

She looked ahead to see how far they were from the hospital, then met Shane's gaze in the rearview mirror. She saw something in his look, something deep, something confusing. Her senses reeled with an answering emotion. For a moment she was frozen in limbo.

Joanna's next contraction brought Starr's attention back to her friend. When it was over, Jo said, "They're coming closer than ever."

"Yes. You're going to make short work of this,

aren't you? You're going to have this baby in no time at all.''

Shane parked the car near the emergency entrance, then bolted for the hospital. By the time Starr had helped Joanna from the car, he was racing across the pavement pushing a wheelchair. They bustled Joanna inside where they hurried past the woman who signed in new patients. "No time," Starr called. "This baby's on the way now."

They didn't stop until they'd reached the elevator. Starr punched the button for the second floor. After a moment, Shane punched it again. And again.

She understood his irritation. "This old elevator has always been slow as sin." The doors finally slid open.

"Wait a minute!" the receptionist called. "You can't go upstairs without signing in." She ducked inside just before the doors slid shut.

As the elevator crept slowly upwards, the woman jotted information on her form. Joanna gripped the sides of her wheelchair as another contraction overtook her, and Starr cast a look at Shane. The grooves were back in his face. His gaze was intent upon Joanna, poised, ready. His expression was closed to everything except the needs immediately at hand. Then he glanced at Starr, and his expression wavered. She could have become lost in that look.

"The baby's coming!" Joanna gasped.

"Don't push!" Starr ordered. "Just pant."

The elevator doors slid open. Joanna squeezed her eyes shut and began to pant. Starr felt helpless in the face of her friend's pain.

"David . . . won't . . . make . . . it."

A robust nurse with salt-and-pepper hair started

barking orders. She pushed a red button, helped Joanna from the chair, and ordered everyone else to leave.

"Starr . . . don't . . . go."

"I'm not going anywhere, Jo. I'm staying with you."

Shane backed from the room, a feeling of intense helplessness gripping him. And he'd thought undercover detective work was horrifying!

Another nurse bustled into the room, followed by a doctor. More commands were issued and voices mingled with other voices. Then he heard an anguished cry that sent his heart to the pit of his stomach.

It had been a cry of pain.

He turned his back to the doorway and paced from one end of the hall to the other. When he neared the room again, Starr's soothing voice reached him, reassuring, crooning, giving. It sent something unnameable rushing through his body.

What was happening in there? No movie scenario had ever prepared him for this! *No wonder I never had children. No, the reason I never had children was because I never met a woman I wanted to have children with.*

The doctor stated what seemed to be obvious. "There's no time to get her to the delivery room. This baby's coming now."

Starr's sultry voice reached inside his reverie. "Looks like we made it just in time, Joanna."

He vaguely registered the doctor's next words. "Push. That's good." A sound, almost inhuman, followed. Shane cringed. Then there was silence.

A faint cry, barely a sound at all, pierced the quiet. The sound steadily grew into a healthy wail.

"It's a girl!"

Just then a man, looking stricken with fear, burst past Shane into the next room. "Joanna!"

"Oh, David, we have another daughter."

With the backs of her hands Starr swiped at the tears coursing down her cheeks. She stepped away from her friend, making room for David at his wife's side. She took another step back, a smile tilting her mouth, as David kissed Joanna, murmuring words of love. A few moments later the doctor placed the tiny, wet scrap of a baby in Joanna's arms. The smile drained from Starr's face.

She inched back farther, along the perimeter of this family's circle. A knot gripped her heart, a pain so intense she caught her breath. Even in this moment of wonder, Starr doubted Joanna knew how much she had. Most people took *family* for granted.

Not Starr. She had no one. Except Uncle Mick. And he wasn't even hers to have.

Steadily she moved, step by step, until she'd backed through the door, smack into Shane. He spun around, his hands gripping her shoulders to steady them both. She raised her eyes to his. "It's a girl."

"I heard."

She sniffled.

Shane gallantly handed her his handkerchief, which made her giggle and sniffle simultaneously.

"You were wonderful."

She heard the huskiness in his voice, saw the warmth in his brown eyes. She could hardly lift her voice above a whisper. "You managed to get us to the hospital in record time. I promise I'll never complain about your driving again."

"I'll hold you to that."

Gazing into his eyes, she wished she could forget everything else; forget who they were, why he was here, forget about the diary. She wished she could. But she couldn't.

Taking a shuddering breath, she stepped away from him. "Did you finish Hannah's diary?"

His expression sobered; his gaze bored into hers. "Yes."

"And?"

"I want you to read it."

The suspense of the past hour, the past few weeks, was beginning to wear her down. She heard the thread of hysteria in her own voice, but couldn't quite force it away. "Is Mick the father?"

He seemed to weigh his answer carefully. "She doesn't say. Exactly."

"But you think he is."

"What I think doesn't matter."

Just then David came bounding from the next room, a smile as big as Lake Michigan lighting his face. He hugged Starr and shook Shane's hand, mumbling thanks and monosyllables and unintelligible words. He propelled Starr toward the room with something that sounded like, "Joanna, say 'Hi!', so happy."

Starr put on a smile and rushed to Joanna's side. "Jo, I'm so happy for you."

"I never would have made it here in time without you. And Shane."

Starr decided to ignore the reference linking her to Shane. "I guess you showed Maybell. She swore you wouldn't have the baby until the moon was full."

"Well, she did predict we'd have a girl. David and I are going to have to rethink the name 'Matthew.' "

Starr agreed that Matthew was no longer appropriate. She stayed for a few minutes, joking about the telephone call, the ride to the hospital, and the strength of her friend's grip. But through her joy for her friend, pain fell to her stomach like lead. She hugged Joanna and David and touched her palm to the wispy brown hair on the new baby's tiny head. Before her tears overflowed, she turned and fled.

Her gaze darted about the hall, searching for a tall, silent man. Shane was nowhere in sight. Starr walked through the heavy double doors, past the old nurses' station, to the elevator. She gazed at the two buttons, then turned and took the stairs.

She didn't stop until she'd reached the door to Uncle Mick's room. Taking a deep, steadying breath, she pushed through. He turned when she entered, and grasping the edge of the bed for support, he declared, "I told you I wouldn't need to use a walker."

Starr rushed to her uncle. She slid her arms around his waist and buried her face in his flannel robe. He smelled of pipe smoke and home.

He grasped her with one hand, murmuring, "Lass, what is it?"

She loosened her hold on his waist and let her arms fall to her sides. "Joanna just had her baby. She couldn't reach David so she called me. We barely got her here in time for the birth. A healthy seven-and-a-half pound girl."

"A girl, aye?"

Starr nodded, remembering the diary, remembering that Hannah, too, had once had a baby girl. Shane believed that child had been Mick's daughter. Was Mick thinking that very thought?

She felt on the verge of bursting with anxiety. She had a sudden trembling need to flee from Uncle Mick's probing gaze, to run, to never stop.

The hand at her shoulder drew her gaze. Mick's brown eyes, crinkled with age, gazed into hers. "Lass, you look tired. Let's sit."

Like a child, she obeyed.

"Joanna isn't the only reason for the circles beneath your eyes, is she?" When Starr didn't answer, he continued. "Who did you mean when you said *we* just now?"

She didn't meet his eyes. "Shane and I."

"Aye. Just as I thought. You're thin, lass. And tired. I'll be out of here in a few days. I never should have asked you to find *my* answers."

"They've become *my* answers, too, Uncle Mick. So don't worry about me. I just can't wait to have you back home."

Mick tactfully changed the subject, telling her how anxious he was to see the rooms she'd painted and complaining about the nurses. Starr relayed some of the village gossip and told him about Trixie. The subject of Shane Wells didn't arise. But he was there, in the back of their minds. He was already hovering between them.

After her visit with Uncle Mick, she peeked in to see Joanna, who was now settled into a room with her newborn daughter. She ran into Jo's brother and sister-in-law in the lobby and Maybell at the front door.

"Didn't I tell her it would be a girl?" May gushed.

Starr didn't mention the fact that her due date had been two weeks off the mark. Neither did May.

"You look exhausted, Starr. The girls are coming to my house for baked lasagna. We'd love it if you'd join us. You can tell us exactly what happened with Joanna. I want to hear every single detail."

Starr didn't relish the idea of returning to Mick's empty house. As she pictured the diary which waited on the table, her stomach rumbled with hunger. "I'd love to come to supper, Maybell." She knew she was postponing the moment of truth. But as weariness washed over her, she didn't care. The truth could wait a little while longer.

Hours later she trudged through the door and into the brightly lit kitchen. Darkness had fallen outside. It matched her sullen mood. Trixie met Starr with boisterous barks. She let her out, then waited for her scratch at the door. Ignoring the diary, she walked into the bathroom where she bent to plug the drain and turn on the taps.

Once again, she slid down into the swirling bubbles. This time she didn't bother with her hair. It floated, unchecked, around her submerged shoulders. Starr sank back against the tub and closed her weary eyes.

A tiny drop of water dripped from the tip of the faucet, but Starr hardly noticed. When the water began to cool, she tugged the plug from the drain and stood. She dried with one of the new towels, then donned her royal blue gown and soft robe.

The floor creaked beneath her step. She barely heard. She walked to the kitchen table where she grasped the diary in both hands. The day of reckoning couldn't be put off forever.

She tucked her feet underneath her in Uncle Mick's favorite chair and opened the diary. The table lamp cast soft light into an otherwise dark room. Trixie fell asleep on the rug on the floor. And Starr read on.

Hannah's words came to life, so vibrant and young, so filled with love. And as Starr read Hannah's thoughts, she began to feel a bond with a woman long dead.

June 22, 1942

Mother is growing weaker, and my worries increase each day. I listen with dread and sadness as Mick and Jake speak of the war. Jake has already served our country, his narrow escape at Pearl Harbor and the slow recovery of his injured leg a constant reminder of the dangers and horror of this war. I fear Mick will join in the fight against Hitler. It is only June yet I feel my summer is nearly over.

June 29, 1942

I met Mick in the tower tonight. We gazed at the stars, then walked along the shore in the moonlight. I've never known a man like him. Good to his soul. Gruff. And gentle.

Starr paused in her reading. Hannah could have been describing Shane, a grandson she hadn't even dreamed of yet, a grandson she would never meet.

July 3, 1942

Tonight I became a woman.

Starr's mouth went dry. She smoothed a fingertip over the peace signs at the end of her chain as she continued. The next few entries were filled with

Mick, with laughter and love, with carefree days and star-filled nights.

July 25, 1942

Mick is leaving. I don't know how I will bear being separated from him for even a day. My heart feels like breaking.

August 3, 1942

Mick is gone, gone to fight on the ocean so far away. I miss him so. Jake has become a beacon in my storm. He is a dear friend.

August 10, 1942

Oh, what will I do? I cannot think through this haze of tears. Mother is so ill. How can I disgrace her and Father?

August 20, 1942

Mother's condition is growing worse. Father and Mother are returning to Shelby. Jake, so quiet and strong and sincere, has asked me to marry him and I have accepted. After this child is born, we will go back to Shelby to help Father in the store. Now I must not look back. However, I'll never forget the summer of my seventeenth year.

Starr slowly lowered the diary to her lap. A lone tear crept down her cheek, hovered at her chin, then dropped to a blank page in Hannah's diary.

In her heart she knew. Mick had loved Hannah and she him. Though Hannah hadn't written it in words, Starr knew she'd carried a child back to Shelby. Mick's child.

She placed the diary next to Mick's pocket watch

on the stand by his chair. A hollow emptiness began to close around her as she gazed at those two items.

She jumped to her feet, startling a surprised *yip* from Trixie. "It's all right, girl. Go back to sleep."

There was only one place Starr could go to think. She let her robe and gown fall to the floor in her room, dressed, then hurriedly put Trixie in the kitchen, took the lighthouse key from the peg behind the kitchen door, turned, and slipped into the night.

She parked her car beneath the trees near the old gate behind the lighthouse. Clouds periodically hid the moon and stars from view as she hiked to the lighthouse. The lock clicked open with a turn of the key. She left the key in the lock, then quietly began to climb the stairs.

She hadn't been inside the lighthouse at night since she was barely more than a child. She shone her flashlight all around, then walked to the windows overlooking the lake. The waves looked dark, the water fathomless, as deep as the night. Hannah's words echoed through her mind: *Tonight I became a woman.*

Starr wondered about the young woman Mick had loved; her spirit, the decision to leave Pinesburg with Jake, to leave Mick in the past. In those times and circumstances, Starr knew Hannah had no real choice.

So, Shane *was* Mick's true grandson. And she was simply an orphan he'd taken in. Oh, she knew Uncle Mick loved her. But he now had *real* family.

Shane hurried past the car parked beneath the dilapidated No Trespassing sign, fear's icy fingers gripping his insides. *Didn't she realize it was dangerous to come here at night?*

With the silence of the wind, he drew the picklock from his pocket. In the darkness he felt the key in the lock and scowled. *Why didn't she send up a flare or hire a band to broadcast her whereabouts?* He closed the door quietly, then turned the lock against intruders in the night.

With painstaking patience he took the stairs. At the top, he stopped. She stood gazing into the distance. He wondered if she saw the lake. Or was she imagining what Mick and Hannah had seen so long ago? Her shoulders were slouched in defeat. He would have given his last dollar to lift her anguish away.

"Starr."

She didn't turn, didn't answer.

He strode to her side. "You shouldn't be here."

"Because you're Mick's grandson?"

He swore under his breath. "Because it could be dangerous."

She turned her eyes to his. With only the light of the half moon, they looked as dark as the night, flecked with a single moonbeam. Even in the darkness, he read pain in her eyes. Terrible regrets assailed him. He shouldn't have come; not to this lighthouse, not to this town.

He looked out across the dark water, into the star-filled night. Once again he wished he believed in wishes made upon stars. If he did, he'd wish her pain away.

He was a man unaccustomed to reaching out. Yet he wanted to reach out to her. But how? What could he say? What could he do? Shane saw her shiver in the darkness and raised his hand to her hair. The curling tendrils felt cool and damp against his palm.

The scent of roses wafted to his nostrils. When his fingers splayed deeper into the softness he watched her lashes flutter down at his touch.

He pulled her to him, and she turned her face into the collar of his leather jacket. He silently offered his body's heat to warm her. She held herself so still in his arms, as if she didn't have enough energy to move. He kissed her temple. The sigh that followed squeezed into his heart.

A noise from below broke the silence. The door opened, then thudded closed. A sharp reprimand followed. He felt her stiffen in his arms, but didn't let her go. He placed a finger to her lips, then automatically reached to his side for the gun he no longer carried.

"Don't move," he whispered.

Gruff voices and occasional words drifted to their ears, words about shipments and payment. After what seemed like an eternity, the door closed and the lighthouse once again was quiet.

From the vast windows above, Starr and Shane watched the shadows of two men creep through the darkness. Moonlight glinted off one man's silver ponytail. Shane wondered how many gray haired men in these parts wore their hair in a ponytail. Once again the men boarded two separate boats, then rowed a good distance from shore before starting the motors.

"Starr, promise me you'll stay away from here," he whispered. They both watched until the lights disappeared in the distance. She didn't answer. He wondered if she was really stubborn enough to come here alone, at night, knowing how dangerous it could be.

She came here tonight. He let all his breath out in a long, loud sigh. *She'd come here again.*

Before those men had arrived, Shane had been about to tell Starr he was leaving. He had no place to go, no one to go to. But he couldn't bear seeing the spark die from her eyes.

Now he couldn't leave. Her safety depended on his staying. He'd stay . . . until he figured out who was using the lighthouse. He'd stay . . . until he was certain Starr was safe.

Leaning forward, he whispered, "Have you asked anyone about that stray dog's owners?"

Criminals had just broken into the lighthouse, had carried on a conversation about payment and shipments. *Crooks* had been in Uncle Mick's lighthouse! And Shane wanted to know if she'd found out who Trixie belonged to? "No." Her voice died away on that single syllable.

"Good. When you do, I'd like to go with you. Maybe someone will say something. Maybe someone's seen something. Or someone."

Shane held the flashlight while she locked the heavy door. Starr hoped he didn't notice the tremor in her fingers. When they neared her car, she dug her keys from her jacket pocket. Shane reached for them, but Starr jerked them away.

"It's been a long day, Starr. I'll drive you home."

"I'm perfectly capable of driving myself!" She knew she sounded indignant, maybe even a little childish. Her eyes challenged him to make something of it.

"I know you're capable. I want to do this for you, that's all."

She gripped the keys in her hand, the pressure

leaving a key-shaped impression in her palm. "Why did you come to the lighthouse tonight?"

"I felt restless so I went for a walk. Why? Do you think I'm involved with those other men?"

She'd never given that a thought. She thought about it now. He *had* been there both times those men had come. But then, so had she. Her fingers opened slowly and she dropped the keys into his outstretched hand. "No. I don't believe you're involved with them."

"Why?" His voice held a challenge.

They slid onto the seats in her car. He didn't close his door and in the dimly lit interior, she looked into his eyes. *Why?* Good question.

"Because I trust you."

His expression changed from one of intense concentration to something else. The grooves at his mouth deepened. He closed the door and started the engine.

"You didn't answer my question, Shane. Why did you come to the lighthouse tonight?"

He didn't answer her for a moment. The car bumped over the uneven ground. His words, when they finally came, were as bumpy as the lane. "I went there to tell you something."

"To tell me what?"

"It doesn't matter. Those men changed my plans."

Starr wondered what those two men had to do with what he'd been about to tell her. The idea of strangers in their lighthouse made her cringe. "Maybe I should have had the lock changed that first time you picked it."

"Then the criminals would have known someone else frequented the property. I have a better chance of catching them if they don't know about us." He pulled the car into the driveway, then followed her up to the house. "We need to talk. Can I come in?"

She flipped her hair behind her shoulders and nodded.

She saw him look at the table, at the place he'd left Hannah's diary. The table was empty.

"It's been quite a day," he murmured.

"Yes, it has." They'd searched through the light-house, found the diary, witnessed the birth of Joanna's baby, read Hannah's words, and seen the lighthouse intruders, all in one day.

Starr remembered how the baby's tiny head had felt beneath her palm, remembered her small cry. "Newborn babies always make me . . ." She didn't finish.

"You're tired."

She lifted her chin and met his gaze. "If one more person tells me I look tired or too thin, I'll punch him in the nose." Starr watched his eyes travel over her, from her head to her toes. Feelings sprang in each place his gaze rested.

"Tired, maybe. But believe me, that Say Yes to Michigan logo is stretched to perfection."

She became aware of his gaze on her breasts; felt them tighten at his look. "Have you ever wished things could be different, Shane?"

"Yeah. As a kid I wanted my parents back. A few months ago I wanted Jake. I've wished a million times I could have Jazz back." Silently he added, *And right now I wish I could have you.*

"So many people in the past. Do you ever wish your future could be different?"

He closed his eyes against his memories, and she

knew he was thinking about Jake and his parents, of a street kid—a kid he'd cared about, a kid he'd lost. When he opened them, she stepped closer, never taking her eyes from his. Even though she believed he was Mick's grandson, she couldn't deny the way her heart swelled when he looked into her eyes. His nearness was more habit-forming than chocolate, sweeter than candy, more luscious than anything she'd ever felt before.

She wished they could have met under different circumstances. But all the wishing in the world wouldn't change the fact that he was Mick's flesh and blood. All the wishes in the world wouldn't change the fact that she had no one. All the wishes in the world wouldn't give her what Joanna had, what most people took for granted.

Too bad wishes couldn't come true.

Shane watched emotions flit across Starr's hazel eyes. None of them happy. Even with the dark circles beneath her eyes, she looked beautiful. Her hair hovered around her face and shoulders. He knew he shouldn't have come and knew he couldn't leave.

Hannah's diary didn't change anything for him. Not really. He knew who his real grandfather was. But he didn't *know* him. He didn't want to go back to the streets of Chicago. He still had nothing to offer a woman like Starr.

Nothing. Except to keep her safe.

He leaned toward her, inhaling the rose scent of her hair. His lips brushed hers, warm and soft. Before the kiss deepened, he straightened and turned. "Get some sleep, okay? I'll see you in the morning."

NINE

Starr threw the door open to Shane before he'd lifted his hand to knock. It was still early. Lights were popping on in the houses up and down the street as the people inside began their days. They'd planned to take a walk through the village and ask the people they met about Trixie. But she hadn't expected him so early.

In the light of early morning, she noticed the changes in Shane's appearance instantly. Instead of his usual faded jeans, he wore dark olive slacks. She was accustomed to seeing him in his leather bomber jacket, and the tweed sports coat and pale olive shirt he now wore took her by surprise.

"Aren't you a little overdressed for a hike through Pinesburg?" She was scarcely aware of her own voice. Instead, she felt mesmerized by the powerful aura of the man before her. The cut of the sports coat he wore this morning accentuated his size. His hair was now neatly styled, his face clean shaven.

He stepped through the doorway and closed the door without taking his eyes from hers. "There's been a slight change in plans. My captain called first thing this morning. I have to go back to Chicago. I'm on my way to the airport in Traverse City right now."

"To the airport?"

"It's about Jazz. His murderer's attorney is trying to weasel his client out of a life sentence."

"I thought you said he was in prison."

"He is. I have to go back to make sure he stays there."

"But why are you flying? It isn't *that* far to Chicago."

Shane stepped closer. There was something about him this morning, something barely leashed. Her eyes took in his powerful presence, but it was more than just his physical proximity. She watched his gaze stray to her mouth. Something in his eyes held her still.

"Because flying is the fastest possible way to get there and back again."

"I see." She didn't really see at all.

He stepped closer, and Starr tipped her head back to see his face. The fingers that grasped her shoulders warmed her skin beneath her shirt. "I need something from you."

Her eyes raised to his questioning gaze. "What is it, Shane? How can I help?"

His voice lowered until it was little more than a husky whisper. "Stay away from the lighthouse until I return."

"That's all?"

"What do you mean 'that's all'?"

His eyes glinted with irritation, and Starr wet her lips. She wondered if he'd ever answer her questions with a simple explanation.

She raised her hands to his upper arms. The fabric was soft to her touch, the muscles underneath flexed, firm and solid. "Why is it so important to you that I stay away from the lighthouse?"

Shane swore under his breath. Most of the words were unmistakable. He loosened his grip on her shoulders but didn't remove his hands. "Because I don't want anything to happen."

She didn't realize she was holding her breath. For a moment she thought he was going to add *to you*. But then the moment passed.

"Until we know who's using the lighthouse and why, we have to assume they may be armed and dangerous. If you can't promise me you'll stay away, I won't go back to Chicago." Something raw glittered in his dark eyes.

"But you have to go back. For Jazz's sake."

"I don't have to. Jazz . . ."

Starr's heart swelled with feelings for this silent man. She knew he felt he'd let his young friend down. She also knew he wouldn't be able to put it behind him until he was certain Jazz's murderer was behind bars. Permanently.

"All right."

Skepticism raised his voice. "Exactly what do you mean by 'all right'?"

"All right. I'll stay away from the lighthouse. You have my word."

Before she could breathe, before she could think, before she could even blink, Shane kissed her. Hard. His fingers massaged her shoulders, pulling her tight to his body. Her heart seemed to enlarge within her rib cage, where it beat wildly against his chest.

His grip tightened and his breathing became ragged. He delved his fingers into her hair, tipping her head upward. The warmth of his arms was so male, so uniquely Shane. He whispered something unintelligible, and although she didn't understand the words she understood the tone, the desire. For a moment her lips clung to his. For a moment love beat in her heart. As quickly as he'd begun, he ended the kiss, leaving her mouth yearning for more.

With surprising gentleness, he smoothed her hair where his fingers had tangled it. With a half smile she'd come to crave, he declared, "I'll be back as soon as I can."

He turned and left without saying good-bye. But then, he hadn't said hello, either. Starr wondered how long it would take her heart to return to its normal beat. She wondered if it ever would.

Later that evening she roamed about Uncle Mick's house. Since she'd promised Shane she'd stay away from the lighthouse property, she'd busied herself with housework, a tedious task. But she wanted everything to be perfect for Uncle Mick's homecoming when he was released from the hospital tomorrow afternoon.

With the cleaning and polishing finished, she visited Mick and Joanna in the hospital. Both were glowing with happiness that they'd be going home tomorrow. Starr was happy for them. She was! But all day long something nagged at her. Something vague.

That feeling was there when she heard Uncle

Mick's spry chuckle. It was there when she saw Joanna touch her lips to her newborn daughter's tiny
cheek. It was there as she stocked the refrigerator
with fresh food.

As she and Trixie went for a vigorous walk after
supper, the reason for her mood began to dawn on
her. It wasn't until she went back to the hospital
to see her uncle that she finally realized what was
wrong.

Uncle Mick was coming home tomorrow. She'd
have to show him Hannah's diary and he'd know
Shane was his flesh and blood. She didn't know how
much longer she'd have Mick to herself; she didn't
know how much longer she'd have him at all.

That uncertainty made her restless. She'd lost
count how many times her fingertips had strayed to
her mouth, where her lips still tingled from Shane's
kiss. Restless? *Restless was too mild a word.* She'd
felt like bursting out of her skin all day.

Her pacing led her into the bathroom where she
stepped from her clothes. Wearing nothing, she
brushed through her hair, those smooth strokes her
last hope for relaxing. As that tiny droplet of water
gathered at the end of the leaky faucet, then plopped
to the tub below, she closed her eyes. She took a
deep breath, then slowly let it out. In no mood for
her usual bath, Starr stepped beneath the shower.
Finally, she was *beginning* to relax.

The telephone jangled from the kitchen. Her eyes
flew open, and Starr scrambled from the tub. With
water sliding down her body she grabbed a large
towel. She didn't take time to properly dry herself
off. Instead she wrapped the towel around her and

hurried toward the kitchen, her feet leaving wet prints on the worn linoleum floor. `

Shane stared at his reflection in the motel room mirror. After the third ring, he watched the grooves beside his mouth deepen. After the fifth ring, tiny beads of sweat broke out on his upper lip.

Where in the hell was she?

"Hello?"

He recognized that smooth voice, although he'd never heard her sound quite so breathless before. Her voice didn't alleviate his discomfort. It sent heat to areas of his body he was trying to ignore. On a half breath and a prayer, he sputtered, "Thank God!"

"Shane?"

"Were you just getting home?"

"No, I was in the shower."

The sudden image of her all rosy and warm and damp did erotic things to him, made him all the more aware of the uncomfortable fit of his jeans. "I'll hold on if you want to go put something on."

"No, no. This towel's fine."

Another potent image. He remembered the way she'd looked standing in that kitchen wearing nothing but a soft towel. He could almost smell the scent of roses wafting from her damp skin. Shane wished all those miles didn't separate them. He wished she was standing before him in this very room. If she was, he'd let that towel fall to the floor, let his hands glide down her smooth skin, down to her slender waist, over the slight rounding of her narrow hips. Then they'd stray to her stomach and up, up . . .

"Shane, are you there?"

The worry in her voice pulled him out of his imaginings. "I'm here, Starr." He wished to hell he was some place else. In Mick Mahoney's kitchen would suit him fine.

"Oh."

"I just wanted to say hello." He'd wanted to hear her voice. "Just wanted to make sure you were all right."

He wanted a helluva lot more than that.

"I'm fine. How are you?"

"Couldn't be better." He shook his head at his reflection in the mirror. *I wonder how long it'll be before she starts talking about the weather.*

"It was a beautiful day."

He saw the grooves beside his mouth deepen.

"Is Jazz's, er . . . um . . . Is that man going to stay in prison?"

Shane let out a long, slow breath. "Yeah. For a long, long time."

"So you've accomplished what you set out to do."

"Yeah." It was surprising what little pleasure it had brought him. "Have you asked anyone about Trixie?"

"No. I wanted to wait until you came home."

Home. He closed his eyes against the feelings that word evoked. Pinesburg was *her* home. Not his. He had accomplished what he'd intended in Chicago. But in the process he was more certain than ever that he didn't want to come back here, to this city, to this work. He was a man without a purpose, a man without a home.

I can't explain the reason for my desire to hurry back to Pinesburg. He grimaced at the word *desire.*

"Shane?"

"Yes?"

"I have to go. I'm freezing."

Once again he imagined her standing in the middle of that old-fashioned kitchen wearing nothing more than a terry bath towel. He also imagined what goose bumps would be doing to her body underneath that towel. How he'd like to warm her. "Go put some warm clothes on, Starr. I'll see you in the morning."

"In the morning?"

"Yes. I'm taking the first puddle hopper out of here."

Starr's soft chuckle expanded his heart, among other things.

"Good-bye, Shane. Sleep well," she murmured.

"Night, Starr."

Shane left Starr in the car with Trixie, then disappeared inside the hardware store. A few minutes later he returned with a bright red leash dangling over his arm. He leaned over the seat to fasten the leash to Trixie's collar. When he reached his hand toward the dog, Trixie bared her teeth, backed into the farthest corner, and growled.

Shane had encountered more than his fair share of physical pain in his life, but that didn't mean he liked it. And being bitten by an angry dog was not on his agenda for the day. Trying again, he slowly reached his hand toward the dog, who in turn bared her teeth once more.

"Oh, for chrissakes!" he sputtered. "She won't let me anywhere near her."

"Here. I'll try," Starr replied. He thrust the leash to the seat and scowled. She took the leash and with a soft, soothing voice, calmed the dog, then fastened the clip to Trixie's collar.

"Oh, Shane, don't take it personally. We don't know what she's been through. Maybe her previous owner was a man. Maybe he abused her. Maybe that's why she doesn't like you. Not that she *doesn't* like you."

He knew she was teasing. It twinkled in her eyes and tipped her mouth into a silken grin, which in turn pulled his insides into a tight knot. He could see the dusting of blusher on her cheeks, the color of strawberries on her full lips. Her lashes were darkened to almost black. But it was more than just makeup that intensified her beauty. The dark circles beneath her eyes were nearly nonexistent. His absence seemed to have been good for her.

"You look better this morning, Starr."

"If that's your idea of a compliment, forget it."

Her caustic tone made him examine his statement. The silence between them grew as he studied her expression. "I meant that as a compliment, even if it didn't sound like one. You look rested. Beautiful."

He watched the warmth of his sincerity soften her gaze. "Thank you. After everything that's happened these past few days I didn't expect to sleep at all. But I did. Like a baby. I don't think I even moved for over eight solid hours. It was heavenly. And you?"

Shane had spent more than his share of nights drinking strong coffee to stay awake on a stakeout or while creeping through the shadows of the Chicago streets. But last night had been different. He'd lain awake staring at the ceiling, listening to the night sounds inside the motel. He kept imagining Starr was lying with him. He could practically feel her smooth skin, smell her rose-scented skin.

After hours of tossing and turning, he'd tried to think of ways to keep her safe. Instead his thoughts had been filled with ways to touch her, and the sheet became a tangled mass at his ankles.

He'd slept on trains, on cement floors, in alleys, sitting up or lying down. Hell, he could practically sleep standing, freezing cold, or stifling hot. But there was one physical condition that refused to allow him to sleep.

The cold shower he'd taken at 3 A.M. had alleviated his discomfort, but the effects had been only temporary. Besides, cold showers had never been conducive to sleep. Neither had worry. Nor unspent desire.

"Come on, baby, let's go," she crooned.

Shane caught his breath at the endearment. But when he turned his head he saw that Starr's gentle voice and soft smile had been for Trixie. He swallowed his disappointment that her endearment had been too.

"Are you ready, Shane?" Starr brought her attention from Trixie to stare into Shane's eyes, wondering if he'd heard her question. It wouldn't be the first time he didn't answer, and she doubted it would be the last. His expression was closed to her inspection, as if he were guarding some deep, private emotion. She hesitated, measuring him for a moment, then opened her door.

She pushed the front seat forward for the dog, then grasped the leash with both hands. The way Trixie pulled, first one way and then the other, it was pretty apparent she wasn't accustomed to being on a leash or chain.

"Whoa, Trixie. Hurry, Shane." Starr started up the sidewalk, being pulled by a skinny black dog who seemed to know exactly where she was going.

Matt Dearling, the owner of Pinesburg Hardware, was raising the awning outside his store. Starr stopped for a moment to ask if he'd seen the dog before. Mr. Dearling paused and said, "No, can't say that I have."

When Trixie barked at the man Starr cast a look in Shane's direction, willing her eyes to say, *See? I told you it wasn't* you *in particular she didn't like, but men in general.*

Trixie strained against the leash and Shane took the cord, Starr's hand and all, in his. With his touch, a shudder passed through her. Her body answered his contact with an increased thudding of her pulse.

"Good-bye!" Starr called to Mr. Dearling, and with Shane's firm hand they managed to hold Trixie to a fast walk—straight to Maybell's store.

The April morning sun brightened May's white hair to an almost ethereal color. Her red smock covered her ample body as she waved good-bye to a customer, and Starr knew the exact moment Maybell noticed Shane's hand covering her own.

"Well, Starr and Shane. Fancy seeing you here this morning. Together."

"Beautiful day for a stroll, wouldn't you say, Mrs. Atkinson?" Shane asked.

Starr watched as the tone of Shane's voice worked its magic on Maybell. The older woman's blue eyes widened in appreciation of more than the man's sheer size. "Why, everybody around here calls me May or Maybell. I'd like it if you did, too," she declared, eyeing their entwined hands.

Shane loosened his hand on the leash, then let it go completely. When Trixie threatened to pull Starr right out of her shoes, he covered her hand with his. Without saying a word, he'd shown Maybell that, rather than holding hands, he and Starr were holding Trixie. Meanwhile Trixie skittered this way and that, pulling against the restraining cord.

"Why, just look at her," Maybell teased. "She wants to go back through the alley to see Brutus again."

"Again?" Starr and Shane said in unison.

"Land sakes, yes. She spent a couple of days with my Brutus over two weeks ago."

"A couple of days?" Starr didn't think she liked where this conversation was headed.

"Well, it was love at first sight. And you know me, Starr, I'm not one to interfere with love. Of any kind."

Shane squeezed her fingers. When she looked up at him, he tried to look innocent. But she could have sworn he was enjoying this.

"I would have thought this little scrap of a dog was too weak to, ah, dance in the moonlight with my Brutus. But she wasn't. Came lookin' for him, she did. What was Brutus to do?"

"Poor fella." His comment cost him a sharp nudge in the ribs from Starr's elbow.

"That's what I thought. I'd just put him on his chain to, um, take care of his business. When I went back out to get him he was engaged in . . . well, let's just say I went back inside to award them a little privacy. Let's face it, Starr, a man is no match for a woman in love.''

Starr had no idea what compelled her to meet Shane's gaze. His brown eyes were hooded in sensuality. He smiled at her, as smug as a self-satisfied devil.

She jerked her gaze to May's. "So, Trixie's more than likely going to have pups.''

"If Brutus had anything to say in the matter, yes. She stayed right here for several days. A pretty little thing, isn't she?''

Starr felt, more than heard, Shane's *hmmph!*

"Maybell, do you know where this dog came from? Before she, ah, visited Brutus?'' Starr asked.

"Never saw her before. If she belonged to anyone around here, I'd know it.''

Yes, Starr believed she would.

Starr watched Shane dive into action. He was about as subtle as a freight train. "You're very astute. If there was something going on around here, you'd know it, wouldn't you?''

"You bet I would. That poor dog must be a stray,'' Maybell answered matter-of-factly.

"Starr's getting attached to the animal. You haven't seen anyone else around here? Someone who might have lost their dog or dumped her off? Maybe a man with a long, silver ponytail?''

"Not a soul. You're the only newcomer, Shane. Are you thinking about staying on awhile?'' She made it a point to eye their entwined hands, clasped around Trixie's leash.

"Maybe for a little while.'' Before Starr's eyes, his devilish satisfaction was replaced with a deliberate blankness. If she'd expected a definite yes or no, she was disappointed.

A cold shiver settled over her. She knew only one thing. Whether Shane stayed or left, her life was never going to be quite the same.

The bell on Maybell's door jingled. Eyeing her customers, she said, "I've gotta run. But before I go, tell me, Starr, when is that ornery old sea dog getting out of the hospital?"

That brought a smile to Starr's lips. Ornery sea dog, indeed. When she thought about it, she decided it probably took one to know one. "This afternoon. They're releasing him right after his afternoon physical therapy."

"Wonderful. Now tell me, Starr, have you heard what Joanna and David are going to name the new baby?"

"Jo called me last night . . ." She looked up at Shane, remembering another phone call she'd received the previous evening.

May didn't wait for Starr to finish. "Sydney! I've never known anyone to name a girl Sydney. Oh, well. She's coming home today, too. And mark my words, little Jennifer's going to have her nose put out of place by that new baby. Spoiled rotten, that one is."

Starr hurried to defend her friend. "She's not spoiled, Maybell. Just loved, secure." There must have been something in her tone, a hint of insecurity in her words, because Starr found both Maybell and Shane gazing at her.

Maybell tilted her head to one side and patted Starr's shoulder. "Mick loves you, too, Starr."

Starr looked from Maybell to Shane. She was

saved from responding when Trixie suddenly yanked on the leash. Without another word, she and Shane resumed their search for Trixie's rightful owner.

For the first time since she'd come back to Pinesburg, Starr felt that everything was as it should be. The reason for this sense of rightness was sitting in his old recliner, listening to the weather report for this area of Lake Michigan. Trixie, who had taken a surprising liking to Uncle Mick, was sound asleep at his feet.

But Starr knew her sense of security wouldn't last forever. In her bedroom she brushed through her hair until the curls relaxed into soft waves from her head all the way down to the middle of her back. She then fastened the sides up with a single beaded comb. An old forties' ballad played on the radio in the front room. She wondered if Mick had listened to that song years ago. With Hannah.

Starr looked at herself in the mirror, then took the small diary from the dresser. Uncle Mick had asked her to find the truth about that long-ago summer. It was time to show him what she'd discovered. The moment of truth had arrrived.

Her uncle turned, and Trixie raised her head at the sound of creaking linoleum. She smiled at them both from the doorway.

"I've missed those creaks." Mick's deep voice brought a lump to her throat.

She remembered the way those creaks had alerted her to Shane's presence in the kitchen last week. "They definitely make it impossible for anyone to sneak up on us, don't they?"

"That they do. What do you have there, lass?"

Starr looked down into Mick's warm brown eyes, eyes so much like Shane's. She leaned forward, tilting her head toward him as she extended her hand to his. "It's a diary, Uncle Mick. Hannah's diary."

Something passed through his gaze, something deep, something powerful. The lump in her throat grew.

"Shane and I found it hidden beneath a tile in the floor at the lighthouse cottage."

"You *and* Shane?"

"Yes."

"What does it say?" he asked, his gaze steady, his voice deep.

She watched as his old callused hands rubbed across the leather cover, wishing she knew what to say. She took his glasses from the chair-side table, then handed them to him. "I understand why you loved her. I'd like to have known her too."

Starr took a deep breath, trying to instill happiness into her voice. She leaned down to brush her lips over her uncle's lined face. "I'm going to stop in at Joanna's for a little while. I won't be late."

Mick grasped her hand before she'd straightened completely. He stared into her eyes without letting her fingers go. "Thank you, lass."

Starr turned away then, before the tears she was blinking away could fall.

TEN

Starr felt transparent beneath Joanna's watchful gaze. She wanted, more than anything, to confide in her best friend. But as the minutes ticked away, it became increasingly apparent that there wouldn't be time for confidences between friends. She only hoped her composure didn't appear as fragile as it felt.

While Jo nursed Sydney, Starr welcomed the numerous interruptions from Jennifer, who wanted Starr to read her a story one minute, then tried to pull her into the little girl's bedroom the next. It kept Starr's mind off Uncle Mick and Shane. Almost.

"Jennifer," Joanna soothed, "maybe Starr doesn't want to play with you right now. Why don't you come sit over here with me and your new sister?"

"No!"

Starr and Joanna exchanged a look.

"It's all right, Jo. I'd love to see Jennifer's room."

Ten minutes later, after she'd been introduced to

the three year old's numerous stuffed animals and favorite toys, David appeared in the doorway, informing his daughter it was time for bed.

"I want Mommy to put me to bed!"

"All right. After we get you into your pajamas, Mommy and I will both tuck you in."

"No. I want Starr to help me put on my jammies."

David turned pleading eyes to Starr, who in turn smiled and nodded. "No one's ever going to push you around, are they, Jennifer? Come here and Auntie Starr will help you."

"No. I want Daddy to."

Starr left David to his firstborn and went back into the living room where Joanna was trying to coax a burp out of her fussing infant.

"Has Jennifer been like this all day?" Starr asked.

Joanna smiled indulgently. "I'm afraid so. She doesn't quite know what to think of her little sister." A most unladylike sound erupted from Sydney, and Joanna smiled again, then pressed her lips to the baby's temple. "Would you like to hold Sydney?"

Starr nodded, then leaned to take the tiny bundle from her mother's arms. A gentle ache settled around her heart and tears stung the backs of her eyes. "Maybell's still clucking over your choice of name for your new daughter."

Joanna laughed. "Good."

Starr lowered herself into a nearby rocking chair. The baby was so tiny, it hardly felt like she was holding anything at all.

"There should be a law against anyone's stomach being *that* flat! I can't wait to have a waistline again and lose some of this fat." Joanna puffed her cheeks out in exasperation.

"You just had a baby, for heaven's sake. And you didn't put on much extra weight. That's just baby fat."

"You sound like Maybell!" Joanna declared.

"Bite your tongue!" Starr protested.

Their eyes met in companionable silence a moment before the two friends laughed in unison. Starr looked down at the baby in her arms. "She's beautiful, Jo."

"Starr, what is it? What aren't you telling me?"

The baby's face puckered up as she began to cry and Jennifer's wails became increasingly louder as David entered the room with the three year old on his hip. Joanna took one look at her two daughters and burst into tears. David looked totally bewildered as he turned, first to his wife, then to each of his little girls.

Joanna swiped at her tears and whispered, "Postpartum blues." She reached for the crying infant and David carried a whimpering Jenny to the sofa where the family huddled together. After a few moments, the crying ceased and Joanna and David exchanged a loving look.

Starr didn't belong. She felt it all the way down to her toes. She knew Jo loved her. But this was Joanna's *family*. And this was their moment. She grabbed her purse and jacket, said good-bye, and was out the door before fresh tears could form.

The sky had darkened to the color of black pearls. Starr tipped her head back to gaze at the heavens. Although she couldn't see them, she knew a thick blanket of clouds completely obliterated the moon and stars from view.

Little more than thirty minutes had passed since

she'd left Uncle Mick with Hannah's diary. Thirty minutes wasn't long enough to finish reading and absorb the implication that Shane was indeed his grandson. Starr wasn't sure a lifetime would be long enough.

Looking around her at the familiar town she called home, she tried to think of a place, any place, to go. She couldn't go home. She couldn't go to the lighthouse. And Joanna was busy with her own family. With a hollow feeling Starr realized she had no place, no one.

A pebble skittered across the sidewalk as she began to walk to her car. A dog barked in the distance, and a car turned the corner behind her. Starr pushed her hands deep into her pockets and tucked her chin into her collar, trying hard not to feel sorry for herself. She wasn't very successful as she closed the door and turned the key in the ignition.

Her radio was tuned to a light rock station and Starr listened to a Bette Midler song. The tune usually made her feel good inside, as if someone really *was* watching her from a distance. But not tonight. Not another soul was in sight and Starr couldn't remember feeling so alone, so lonely.

As she approached the Kearn cabin, she took her foot from the accelerator. For reasons she didn't fully understand, she slowly pulled into the driveway behind Shane's car. Light shone from one window, and as Starr gazed at the soft illumination she felt like a weary traveler, bone tired and hungry. Not physically, but emotionally.

She stood on the gravel driveway, trying to decide what to do. She was totally alone. So was Shane.

Maybe, for just a few minutes, they could assuage their loneliness together.

"Hasn't anyone ever warned you the bogeyman will get you if you don't watch out?" Shane stepped from the shadows of the tall maple trees.

His voice conjured up emotions, as smooth and dark as the black pearl sky. Starr turned her head toward the sound, her heart jumping in her chest. But not out of fear. Her heartbeat had accelerated at the sensuous texture of his voice.

Shane's quiet footsteps crunched in the gravel, then stopped just inches from her. Warmth radiated from his body; her own body softened in response.

"I'm not afraid of the bogeyman." No, she was afraid, terrified, of being alone, totally alone, for the rest of her life.

"I remember."

Standing there in the quiet night, Starr felt the heat of his gaze. Like a moth drawn to a flame, his simple words drew her nearer.

She was aware of him—as a man, a wonderful, complex man—and for a moment was too emotion filled to speak. But words strummed through her mind, through her heart. She loved him, this intense, silent, rugged man who'd seen more than any man should see.

She loved him.

The night was incredibly still, as if the invisible stars in the heavens stood silently waiting. She imagined she could hear the waves on Lake Michigan, but in reality, it was only the thudding of her own heart.

Faint rays of light from the nearby window cast Shane's shadowy features in soft illumination. Starr wasn't sure how long she stood there, staring into his eyes. It could have been minutes; it could have been no more than a heartbeat.

A cool breeze lifted her hair. She shivered in the night, but not only from the cold.

"Would you like to come inside where it's warm, Starr?" His smooth voice sent tingles down her body. Without taking her gaze from his, she nodded. Neither said another word as they walked, side by side, up the wooden steps and into his cabin. His silence stoked a gently growing fire within her, until she thought her heart might burst with feeling.

The last time she'd been inside this cabin sunlight had shone through the windows, exposing sturdy, cluttered, unmatched pieces of furniture. Tonight a single bulb cast soft light through the veil of its ancient shade, throwing the entire room into semi-darkness.

They walked further into the room where the furniture was cloaked in shadows. Shane stopped a step behind Starr, then gestured to the clutter. "I wasn't expecting you tonight, Starr."

"I know. But I had nowhere else to go."

Shane closed his eyes as her soft voice penetrated his heart. Without touching her, he moved closer. When she turned her head, her hair touched his face, tickling his chin. He brought his fingers to his face with the intention of brushing the curls away. But that one touch was his undoing.

He sifted his fingers through the softly waving tendrils, not quite certain if he leaned ahead or if she leaned back, because the next thing he knew, her body rested along the entire length of his.

With his fingers still in her hair, he gently brought

her head to his shoulder before his arms encircled her from behind, one hand at her waist, the other slightly higher, at her rib cage. Her breasts rested softly along his forearm, and it was sheer willpower alone that kept him from bringing his other hand up higher, to touch, to caress.

How could he have thought his insides were dead? She was soft, woman soft; and he was hard all over. He'd never felt more alive than at this moment.

His arms tightened around her, and she folded her arms over his, locking herself in his embrace. Her curves molded to the contours of his hard body and desire unlike anything he'd ever experienced pulsed through him.

"I'm glad you came to me." His voice was nothing more than a husky whisper close to her ear. He felt her body begin to melt, to soften to his. He kissed her temple and felt her melt a little more. He wanted her, more than he'd ever wanted anyone or anything in his life. But she wanted, needed, permanence, a future. He couldn't give her those things. He had nothing to offer, no job, no plans for the future.

"Ah, Shane, you're so warm, so incredibly warm," she whispered. Her words drained him of his willpower, making him painfully aware of his warmth, his heat, his desire. He'd thought he could keep her safe. Nothing more. Now he realized he could give her warmth. And pleasure.

Starr held her breath in anticipation of his next move. She knew he was affected by her nearness, could feel his desire against her. For a moment he didn't move, didn't further their contact. Or lessen it.

Confusion flashed in her mind. She'd come back to Pinesburg prepared to help Uncle Mick regain his strength. Instead she'd fallen in love with Mick's grandson.

That he *cared* about her she had little doubt. That he *desired* her, she had none whatsoever. But he didn't *love* her.

She had no one.

Starr straightened, trying to pull from Shane's arms. But he didn't let her go. Instead, he turned her to face him, then framed her face with his big hands, sliding his fingers over her cheekbones, over the delicate curves of her ears.

As she tipped her head back to gaze into his eyes, she was glad he hadn't let her go. She didn't want to leave, didn't want to be alone, if only for this short time.

Passion rose in her at the possessive glint in his eyes. She raised her palm to his cheek, touched a fingertip to the groove at his mouth, then glided her fingers across his lips. Starr felt as though she possessed an enormous power when that groove deepened, when he groaned into her hand.

She slid her fingers into his hair, then rose on tiptoe to press her lips to his. A sound escaped from some place deep inside him. His fingers left her hair, and his hands were suddenly at her back, pulling her hard against him with a force that drew the air from her lungs. Her eyes fluttered closed and she made a sound, half sigh, half moan, as he deepened the kiss. Her hands slid inside his worn bomber jacket, then higher, where she pushed the leather from his shoulders.

He pulled his hands from the sleeves, then tossed

the jacket away, where it landed with a heavy *swish* on the floor. A moment later his fingers found the zipper beneath her chin and her coat was flung in the same direction as his.

Her fingers crept up to his chest where his heart hammered in a wild rhythm. The beat warmed her further, and she pressed her lips to his throat where she murmured his name.

In answer to her touch, to her voice, he swung her into his arms, then strode through a narrow doorway. Without letting her go, his lips found hers and he kissed her until she thought she'd burst with emotion.

Then, slowly, so slowly, he began to lower her feet to the floor, sliding her body down his, one inch at a time, until her feet straddled his. Without putting any distance between them, she stepped out of her shoes, then raised her eyes to his.

The light from the living room didn't penetrate the darkness here. She could make out his shape, nothing more. Her fingertips found the buttons on his shirt. As she began to unfasten the first one, Starr whispered, "Love me, Shane. If only for this one night, love me."

Her words seemed to fuel his desire. She felt his chest heave with his deep breathing, felt his heart quake beneath her hand. Then his lips found hers and she slid her hands around to his back, kneading his taut flesh, reveling in his strength and size.

"Are you sure, Starr? I don't want to hurt you."

Her answer was a passionate thud of her pulse and a soft moan. Starr knew he'd reached the point of no return, and the knowledge filled her with even more longing.

She loved him. Tomorrow didn't matter. They had tonight.

He touched her all over, first through her clothes, then, slowly, painstakingly, utterly passionately, without them. When every last scrap of clothing had been removed and flung to the farthest corners of the darkened bedroom, he pulled her to him, skin to skin, breast to chest, thigh to thigh.

He kissed her until she felt like melting at his feet, then moved his palms down her body from her shoulders to her thighs. Muscles and joints that had felt like melting a moment ago suddenly sprang with new life. With languid agility she moved her body across his, her hands searching, massaging, stroking.

He pressed her backwards until she felt the old chenille bedspread at her back, and inch by inch, the weight of his body covered hers. Coherent thought was replaced with feelings and textures. Shane's muscular arms, a hair-roughened chest, his lean, flat stomach and beard-roughened chin. His long legs and labored breathing, his blatant arousal and the way he murmured her name took her to a new level of intimacy, to a place she'd never gone before.

They moved over the bed, arms and legs entwined, lips clinging, hearts beating, giving pleasure, and receiving it. He covered her breasts with his hands and tiny vibrations spun deep within her body. She was crushed beneath him one moment, sprawled on top of him the next, as their desire built and their hunger intensified.

When their bodies became one, the pleasure was pure and powerful. His heartbeat throbbed against hers and his mouth moved over her own. Small tremors gave way to the greatest bursting of sensations.

Starr cried out his name, then he followed her to that special place.

Sometime later, after their breathing began to return to normal, Starr was filled with a wonderful sense of completeness. Shane kissed her with a gentleness that surprised her after such an intense, anything-but-gentle, heartrending, mind-boggling act of passion.

She smiled against his lips. She couldn't help it. She felt good, darn it, she felt wonderful.

"You are incredible." His voice was still husky, laced with traces of passion. He hadn't said *was*, but *are*.

Starr laughed, deep and throaty. "So are you."

She couldn't see his expression in the dark, could only make out the shape of his head and shoulders. His fingers found her hair, tangled by passion, and smoothed the tendrils off her forehead.

"You should do that more often."

Sensing his look in the darkness, she raised her eyebrow and said, "I beg your pardon?"

"Laugh. Your laugh is marvelous. You should do it more often," he explained.

"Look who's talking."

"Yeah, well . . ." His voice trailed off.

She sensed his hesitation, as if he were about to say, I haven't had a lot to laugh about.

Her heart thudded painfully in her chest. He *would* have. Uncle Mick would make sure Shane had plenty to laugh at in the future.

Starr had had Mick since she was ten years old. Shane's time with his grandfather was just beginning. She'd go back to New York—Shane would stay here. She imagined Mick and Shane, the two men she loved, here in Pinesburg, getting to know one another, finding laughter.

As Starr lay cradled to Shane's chest, listening to the beat of his heart beneath her ear, she understood why she'd come here tonight. This had been her last opportunity to experience this closeness with Shane before he and Mick met. Then they'd be *family*. And she'd be an outsider, just as she'd always been.

Shane sensed her hesitancy, so at odds with her unrestrained passion of only minutes ago. He searched for a way to bring back the closeness they'd just shared. Had he hurt her when he didn't utter words of love?

He'd never said those words to a woman. Never even came close. Until tonight.

But he couldn't utter words of love to Starr. He couldn't offer her anything more than he'd given. And she'd given him so much more in return. The memory of what she'd done to him, how she'd melted in his arms and melted him in return, how she'd moved and tasted and sounded, was increasing the tempo of his heartbeat even now.

And Starr was retreating.

She propped herself up on one elbow and smiled. The moon found a break in the clouds, casting a wan moonbeam across the bed where they lay. Her hazel eyes still glowed with spent desire and such a look of sadness it tore at his heart.

She kissed him, tenderly, with feeling. "I have to go."

"So soon?"

He felt her nod. "I told Uncle Mick I wouldn't be late. I don't want him to worry."

Shane ran his hand down her back, following the

dip in her spine. Goose bumps rose on her flesh in the wake of his touch. She moved her shoulders to escape similar sensations. The action brought her breasts into contact with the hair on his chest. Her body reacted to the sensation. So did his.

"If you have to go, you'd better not keep doing *that*," he whispered.

"Then don't tickle me."

"Oh, Starr, if you'd stay awhile, I could do so much more."

She nipped at his lips playfully, then pulled away. The room grew dark as clouds reclaimed the moon in the sky. "I believe you. But I really do have to go."

She said it with such conviction he couldn't do anything except comply. Sitting at the edge of the bed, she whispered, "It's dark. Would you turn on the light?"

He rolled to his side, then trailed his hand up her back once more. "The bathroom's right through there. I'll gather up our clothes and bring them to you in a minute."

Shane felt her hesitate for a moment, felt her lean into his hand at her back. Then she stood and disappeared through the semidarkness.

He flipped on a light, then pulled on his clothes. Shane bent to retrieve Starr's things from the farthest corners, wispy scraps of satin, soft jeans, her bright pink shirt and matching socks, so bold, so feminine, so much like Starr.

When she emerged from the bathroom fully dressed in those same articles of clothing several minutes later, he couldn't help but remember how he'd whisked them from her body an hour ago. He was tempted to do it all over again.

Starr took a brush from her purse and began to work through the tangles in her hair. "Shane, I seem to have lost the beaded comb I wore in my hair. Did you see it in the bedroom?"

He wished she'd meet his gaze. Instead she averted her eyes and continued to brush her hair into soft waves.

"I'll go look." He found the comb nestled in the hollow of the pillow where her head had rested. Shane clasped it in his hand, then hurried from the room, from his memory of how her hair had felt beneath his fingers, splayed over his pillow.

"Here it is."

"Thanks, Shane." Still she didn't meet his look.

She took the comb from his outstretched hand, then placed it in her purse along with the brush, leaving her hair to wave freely about her face and shoulders. Tucking the purse beneath her arm, she looked ready. Ready to leave.

"Starr."

Finally, her gaze rose to his. For a moment he read tenderness in her look and a trembling awareness and something else, something he couldn't define.

"Uncle Mick will probably call you tomorrow. I'm sure he'll want to meet you, to get to know you." Her statement seemed to cost her a great deal of pain, of uncertainty.

Shane searched for a plausible explanation for the slight quaver in her voice, for her swift retreat. He steadied his gaze on her, but Starr turned away from him, raised her chin, and walked toward the door.

"Good night, Shane." She opened the door, then disappeared into the night.

To Shane, her *good night* had sounded more like *good-bye*.

ELEVEN

When the knock on the front door came, Uncle Mick grasped his cane, then turned to look at Starr. An unmistakable light of anticipation twinkled in his brown eyes. "That'll be Shane."

Starr nodded and moved her mouth into a semblance of a smile, trying to force away the heavy feeling in her stomach. Uncle Mick was anxious to meet his grandson. She didn't blame him. She didn't blame either of them. But that didn't alleviate the ache surrounding her heart.

"Don't get up, Uncle Mick. I'll get it."

She knew she had to open the door to Shane. That in turn would open the door to her memories of last night. She preferred to do that away from Uncle Mick's shrewd gaze.

The sight of Shane standing on the front porch nearly took her breath away. Even with the muscles in her stomach clenched tight, it was impossible to steady her erratic pulse. Shane in the flesh was even more potent than he'd been in her dreams all night long.

"Hello." There was no disguising the intimacy of his deep voice. Her misgivings about being present at this meeting between Shane and her uncle grew with every heartbeat.

"Hi, Shane. Won't you come in?" Starr tried to project an ease she didn't feel. Before her eyes his expression changed. Two lines appeared between his brows, and the grooves at the corners of his mouth deepened. Without moving, he stared into her up-turned face.

"Uncle Mick is looking forward to meeting you, Shane. He's right this way." Only then did he follow her inside.

With the help of his cane, Uncle Mick stood when she and Shane entered the living room. Trixie looked from one human to another, then stood watch at Mick's side. Starr wet her lips and tried to swallow the defeated feeling rising inside. She wasn't certain how to introduce these two men, one a grandfather, the other his only grandson.

Grasping his cane with his good hand, Uncle Mick gestured them closer. "Come here, you two." Starr had no choice but to comply.

Tears blurred her vision when Mick extended his right hand to Shane. "Welcome, lad, it's good to finally meet you."

She stood mutely by as Shane accepted the old man's hand. Fighting back tears, Starr turned to go.

"Would you stay a while, lass?" The plea in Mick's eyes beckoned to her irresistibly.

She looked from Shane to Mick, both pairs of eyes studying her closely. "Of course."

"Have a seat, lad. You too, Starr."

She perched at one end of the sofa while Shane lowered himself to a cushion at the other end. Mick propped his cane on one knee, then took the diary from the table beside his old chair. "Quite a gift." Starr wasn't sure which gift he was speaking of, proof that Hannah *had* loved him, or proof that he did indeed have a grandson.

"You know, Shane, Jake used to lower his eyebrows when he was deep in thought like you are now. You remind me of him." At the younger man's surprised look, Mick added, "Not in appearance, maybe, but there's more to a man than appearance, and you have a piece of Jake in you."

Tears sprang to Starr's eyes and her gaze was drawn to Shane, who stared deep into Mick's eyes. Mick rarely uttered compliments and she realized Jake must have been quite a man to deserve praise after all these years.

"He said I reminded him of you," Shane replied. For a moment the room was completely quiet.

Then Mick slapped the diary against his knee and grimaced in good humor. "You could take that as an insult." The atmosphere in the room seemed to relax.

As her uncle spun tales of his youth, of his friendship with Jake, of humorous pranks and real-life rescues on the Great Lake, Starr watched from the edge of Shane and Mick's fragile, newly formed circle of family. Mick now had *real* family. One that didn't include her. That's what she'd feared from the moment she'd heard of Shane Wells.

The grooves in Shane's face disappeared and his posture, his very stature became less rigid. After a time he stretched his long legs out comfortably, his jeans stretching tight over his thighs. A knot formed in her stomach; she knew precisely the texture of hair on those thighs, the strength in the muscles underneath. She willed her memories away, then listened to her uncle's words. She tried to imagine Mick as a boy, then later as a young man. He would have been very handsome; in that respect he and Shane were alike.

While Shane was totally immersed in his grandfather's tales, Starr stole another glance in his direction. She knew she'd never forget a single detail of his face and wondered what might have happened if they'd met under different circumstances, if he'd been just an ordinary man.

She doubted he'd ever be *just an ordinary man*. Once again her mind turned to last night, which had been anything but ordinary.

Mick's attention was riveted on his grandson and Starr realized Shane was telling her uncle about Kate, Shane's mother. Mick's *daughter*. Jealousy stirred inside her with such force she felt physically ill.

When Trixie scratched at the door, Starr seized her opportunity to escape. She said a hurried goodbye to both men, then grabbed her jacket and Trixie's leash from the peg behind the kitchen door.

Starr allowed Trixie to lead the way and the dog headed straight toward Main Street and Maybell's store. Everyone had someone. Everyone except Starr, that is. Even Trixie had Brutus, May's cocker spaniel.

Jealousy was a new emotion, one she wasn't proud of, but didn't know how to eliminate. It left a bad feeling in the pit of her stomach. The candy bar she bought at May's store didn't alleviate her discomfort. Starr was afraid nothing would.

Shane visited his grandfather often during the next few days. And even if Starr didn't quite meet his eyes, she made certain he couldn't fault her manners or behavior. She was polite and unobtrusive, finding any number of reasons to be away when he arrived.

She took long walks with Trixie, visited with May and "the girls," checked up on Joanna and *her* girls, took Uncle Mick to the hospital every morning and afternoon for his physical therapy, and managed to keep a smile on her face, if only for appearance's sake.

"Yes," she told anyone who inquired. "Shane Wells *is* Mick's grandson. No, Mick hadn't known of Shane's existence until a short time ago. Yes, they're getting along wonderfully." If anyone noticed the stiffness in her shoulders or the tightness in her voice, they made no comment, at least not to her.

The weather report blasted her ears the moment she walked through the back door. Starr unfastened Trixie's leash, then slipped out of her jacket, which she left hanging over the back of the kitchen chair. Uncle Mick's radio was turned up; the somewhat nasal voice of the weatherman was calling for dense fog. With a surreptitious peek into the living room she discovered her uncle, sound asleep in his favorite chair.

On tiptoe she carefully avoided the noisiest squeaks in the floor, although she doubted a creak or two would stir him if the radio broadcast didn't, and headed toward her bedroom. The sight of Shane on his knees in the bathroom froze the smile on her face, froze any thought she'd had that she'd managed to avoid him again.

Leaning over the bathtub, he was fighting with the stubborn plumbing. His jeans stretched tight over his thighs and hips and the muscles in his forearms swelled from exertion. When the wrench slipped he thwacked his knuckles on the exposed pipe. Colorful words poured from his mouth and Starr smiled in spite of herself. She crossed her arms and leaned in the doorway. "Who's winning?"

He swung around. Tipping his head back, he looked up at her, then settled back on his haunches.

Starr watched him move, watched as the muscles in his thighs tightened. Blood raced through her veins as he gave her one of his precious half smiles. "I am."

She noted the blood on his skinned knuckles. "I see." Being careful not to touch him, she wet a washcloth with cool water, then handed it to Shane. Instead of taking it from her, he held out his hand, knuckle side up.

Starr slipped her hand beneath his, palm to palm, then began to dab at the blood with the gentlest of strokes. With his position so near the floor, his face was in direct line of her vision. She hadn't realized she'd stopped dabbing at his skinned knuckles, was only aware of the sensuous glow in his light brown eyes.

She became lost in his look. She'd avoided him like the plague all week. And then, one look, one touch, and her emotions melted. God help her, she wanted him.

With the agility of a much smaller man, Shane

was on his feet, never taking his eyes from hers. A searing pressure filled her lungs as his fingers delved into her hair. With the slowness of a man intent on fulfilling a fantasy, he brought his face closer to hers.

Her eyelids fluttered down the exact instant his lips touched hers. He kissed her, slowly, thoroughly, melting her knees, drugging her good sense, warming her heart, until she ached for more. More kisses, more touches, more closeness.

She slid one hand to the back of his neck, the other up his ribs to where his heart was beating wildly, as wildly as her own. Beneath his thumping heartbeat, she felt a smooth round object through the thin fabric of his pocket.

Starr recognized the size and shape of the object at her fingertips. Uncle Mick's pocket watch, the watch that had been his father's, his grandfather's before that.

A new sorrow replaced the wild beat of her heart and she backed away, breaking the kiss, breaking her connection to Shane. Tears stung her eyes. She lowered her gaze to hide their presence.

Starr felt orphaned all over again.

Before she could turn and run, his fingers grasped her wrist in an iron grip. "He wanted me to have it."

She raised her eyes to his, heard his sharp intake of breath at the tears glistening there. "You deserve to have it, Shane."

"Starr, what is it? Tell me what's wrong."

"Nothing's wrong," she lied.

"Then come here, closer."

"I can't." The words were wrenched past the pain in her heart.

"Why can't you?"

"Because. You're Mick's grandson. You're family."

"But that doesn't matter. You're not blood related to Mick. *We're* not blood related."

She realized he misunderstood her reasoning. "So what you're saying is we're no closer than kissing cousins."

"I'd like to be a lot closer than that, Starr."

"No!" The single word was spoken on a gasp. "I'm leaving in a few days." She had no idea when that decision had been reached. She was as stunned by it as he.

"Why?"

"It's time."

He stared deep into her eyes for interminable seconds. Without uttering another sound, he released her wrist, then turned back to the leaky faucet. She unconsciously smoothed her thumb over the sensitive skin still tingling from his tight grasp, then turned and left the room. Trixie followed her into her bedroom where Starr went down to her knees to hug her pet. The dog stared at her with soulful eyes, then, with tail wagging, licked the tears from her face. Until that moment, Starr hadn't been aware she was crying.

Shane paced from one end of his cabin to the other. Those tears glimmering in Starr's eyes had burned in his chest like a long swallow of cheap whiskey. He knew damn well she hadn't wanted him to see, just as he knew she didn't *want* to leave. He had a feeling she loved him, and the suspicion made him feel raw. People who loved him had a tendency to end up dead.

She said she was leaving. Maybe that would be best for everyone. At least then she'd be safe, as safe as anyone in a big city. He cringed at the thought of her leaving, cringed more at the thought of her staying. What if he couldn't keep her safe? What if he couldn't keep anyone safe?

His thoughts led him through a narrow doorway, the same doorway he'd shouldered through with Starr in his arms. He took a deep breath, then wished he hadn't. The scent of roses, Starr's scent, was still there. The scent of her hair, her skin, seemed indelibly imprinted on his pillow, in his nostrils, in him. The memory of their lovemaking was a cross between a painful knot in his gut and a throbbing hardness somewhat lower. It left him agitated, overheated, uncomfortable. It left him wanting more. But only from her.

And she was leaving. Soon.

Shane strode to a cluttered corner where an old trunk was stashed beneath a battered suitcase and discarded clothing. He brushed the clothing aside and tossed the suitcase onto the bed. Picking it up by the side handles, he carried the trunk to the living room, where he lowered himself to the old couch and opened the lid.

With Jake's passing, Shane had sold Jake's small house, gotten rid of most of the furniture. There hadn't been much to it. Jake never had been one to save things, keep clutter. All Shane had left of the old man was a brittle old rocking chair Hannah had used to rock Kate and Kate had used to rock him. And this old trunk, filled with bits and pieces of the lives of those who'd gone before him. Not much to show for all the love those people had given. Not much at all.

It took a moment for the sound of a hesitant knock on the screen door to penetrate Shane's concentration. He lifted his gaze and his heart thudded in his chest. He'd left the front door open to allow the warm spring breeze entry into the dank old room. Starr's head and shoulders were silhouetted against the bright sunshine.

"It's open, Starr. Come in."

She told Trixie to stay and opened the screen door, letting it bang shut behind her, causing her to jump. It took a few moments for her eyes to adjust to the dim interior, a moment longer for her heart to stop racing at the sight of Shane, sitting on the old sofa, his legs spread apart, knees bent, arms resting on his thighs, hands dangling between them.

"Uncle Mick asked me to give you a message," she whispered, letting him know she wasn't there of her own free will. She'd caught Uncle Mick watching her these past few days, making her jumpy, fidgety, much the way Shane was making her feel now.

"You're out of breath, Starr. Have you been walking?" he asked.

"Yes." But that wasn't the reason for her breathless state. The reason was sitting across the room, a hungry look in his hooded brown eyes, a look she understood, a look she was afraid was mirrored in her own gaze.

"Have a seat." His deep voice sent more feeling racing through her. She looked around her at the cottage clutter, searching for an available chair.

"No, thanks. I can't stay."

"Not even for a minute?" he asked.

She breathed a sigh of relief when his gaze left hers. For the first time she noticed the trunk on the floor in front of him, its lid open, hanging at an angle from old hinges. Starr took a few steps toward him, then a few more. When she was near the trunk, she asked, "What's this?"

Without looking up, he muttered, "A few family mementoes." She'd never heard that tone in his voice, that note of complete aloneness. She went down to her knees and asked, "May I, Shane?" To her dismay, her voice broke, quivering on his name. It drew his gaze, and she couldn't look away.

"Yes."

Her mouth went dry with the desire to reach out to him, to kiss the grooves beside his mouth, to linger, to savor the sensation of her mouth on his. Instead, she tore her gaze from his and delved into the trunk at her side.

She immediately recognized the notes filled with Shane's scrawl, the words Jake had spoken from his deathbed, the words that had brought Shane to Pinesburg, to her. She recalled telling him they were wonderful mementoes to be treasured, but not proof that he was Mick Mahoney's grandson. Terrible regrets assailed her, and she wondered how deeply those words had hurt him.

The trunk wasn't large, the items inside sparse, considering the trunk probably contained all he had left of his loved ones. Except Uncle Mick. For the first time, Starr was glad he had Mick, even if it meant she had no one.

She riffled through several old photographs, listening to Shane spin tales about each one. Since

reading Hannah's diary, Starr already felt a kinship
with the woman. Hearing Shane's tales, as told to
him by his mother and later by Jake, Hannah seemed
even more real. He showed her an old black-and-
white photo of his grandmother as a young woman.
Her hair was long and straight and, although it was
difficult to tell in the photo, was probably dark
blond. She wasn't looking at the camera, didn't appear to be aware of the person taking the picture.
Her eyes held a faraway look, and Starr wondered if
she was thinking about the man she'd loved, and
lost.

Starr realized Hannah hadn't lived to be an old
woman, had died before her thirtieth birthday, not
much older than Starr was now. But Hannah had
loved, hard and strong, honestly and completely.
Could Starr say the same for herself? The *no* flitting
through her mind left her bereft, chased away by a
vehement *yes*. Either way, the answer terrified her.

The next photo was of a chubby baby with unfathomable brown eyes. Shane had been handsome even
then. He looked embarrassed when she told him what
she was thinking, and she had to squash the impulse
to hug him, to wrap her arms around him and show
him how handsome she found him, right here, right
now.

He showed her a portrait of his mother and father,
a handsome couple, Shane held on his father's knee,
Kate nearly an exact replica of Hannah, her mother.
"You're lucky to have this one, Shane. I don't have
any pictures of my parents. They didn't believe in
snapshots. My mother once told me the only true
picture we have is the one we carry in our hearts."

Shane agreed with Starr's mother. No matter how

long he lived, he'd never forget the way Starr looked at that moment, her hair in total disarray, her hazel eyes dreamy, her mouth soft and utterly kissable. The baggy navy sweatshirt she wore had slipped off her shoulder, leaving her creamy skin bare, making Shane aware she wasn't wearing a bra, making him even more aware of his desire.

She reached into the trunk, and he caught a glimpse of her slender collarbone, tarnished peace signs, a smooth breast, its aureole pale brown. At the slightest brush of her arm across her sensitive skin, the center peaked and budded. It would take a stronger man than he to tear his gaze away.

The moment passed, and he heard her voice in the distance, beyond the beating of his heart, his blood pounding in his ears. He tried to concentrate on her words as she talked about her parents and unusual childhood, all the while fighting for willpower, fighting the need to capture her breast in his hand, to pull her to him. To love her senseless.

What would that accomplish? It would relieve the ache in him, relieve the uncomfortable fit of his jeans. But only temporarily.

What would it relieve in Starr? He didn't doubt her passion or his ability to ignite it. She'd quivered in his arms a few nights ago, been in turn both soft and aggressive. He didn't doubt she could be that way again. But what would it prove? What would it settle? She would still leave. And he'd still be left alone.

Despite the breeze blowing through the screen door, the air in the room felt heavy. The locket she held in her fingers slipped to the floor of the trunk as Starr met Shane's look. She let her gaze follow the locket's descent, her eyes resting on a newspaper clipping.

The newspaper photo hardly did the young man, barely more than a boy really, justice. His skin was dark, his black hair cut in the style of the day, flat on top, shaved on the sides. An earring dangled from one ear. And his eyes looked older than time. *Jazz Samuel Johnson. Born February 19,—*

Starr grasped the clipping in both hands and read the youngster's short obituary. "His given name was Jazz?" she asked. Shane nodded.

A feeling of incredible sadness filled her, as if she could feel Shane's despair, his sadness, his guilt. It suddenly didn't matter that strangers were using the lighthouse for a meeting place. It didn't matter that Shane was Mick's true grandson. What mattered was the man sitting before her. What mattered was the look in his eyes, his sadness mixed with desire.

She went up on her knees, fitting her body snugly between his legs, instantly aware of his arousal, of her own desire. She let the paper flutter to the trunk, then slid her hands up his sides to his chest, across his shoulders. For a moment he shuddered with the effort of holding back. Then his arms came around her, crushing her to him, holding her as if he'd never let her go.

She kissed his neck, his throat. With a steadiness that surprised her, she unbuttoned his blue chambray shirt, then pressed her lips to his, letting her palms glide over his chest, down his sides, across his abdomen. She slid her fingertips beneath the waistband of his jeans, then out again, covering his rigid length with both hands.

"Starr," he rasped. "If you want me to be able to stop, you'd better."

"I don't want you to stop. Not now. Not here."

He lifted her to his lap, his big hand finding its way to the inside of her sweatshirt, where he covered her breast, kneaded her swollen flesh, squeezing with just the right amount of pressure, sending tremors down her body to places physically unconnected.

She cried out his name, her lips forming his name, his name forming her lips for another kiss. She grasped the hem of her shirt and lifted it over her head, her hair tumbling about her back and shoulders like a caress. Shane rubbed his hands across her back, spread his fingers through her hair, kissed her with an urgency that made her tremble.

His lips left hers and trailed a path along her jawline, down her neck, across the delicate ridge of her collarbone. He pressed his mouth to the upper curve of first one breast and then the other, before taking a sensitive peak into his mouth.

Starr's fingers delved into his hair, holding his head, moaning his name. When he moved to her other breast, the breeze cooled her wet flesh, sensitized beyond imagination. Her eyelids grew too heavy to support. He shifted, and she became aware of coarse fabric beneath her back.

She managed to open her eyes a crack, and smiled at the look on Shane's face. The tide of passion swirling through her was also taking him by storm. He squeezed to her side, his hands roaming every inch of her body within reach. She deftly unfastened his belt buckle, then used both hands to undo the button and finally lower his zipper.

When she took him in both her hands, he made a

sound so deep in his throat, it was indiscernible in words, but not in intent. With movements that left her reeling, he unfastened her jeans and pushed them out of his way. She adjusted to his weight and gasped as he entered her, his movements primal, consuming, male.

Ecstasy slipped between her lips, flowing from his body to hers. Starr was too emotion filled to speak, and only the deepest of sounds escaped her. Their passion was so uncontrolled, so unforgettable, she wondered if it was of this world. When it was spent, she let her hands fall limply to his back. He framed her face with the gentlest of fingers and kissed her once more.

Trixie's forlorn, soulful howls broke the moment. When it became apparent she wasn't going to stop, Shane swore under his breath and muttered, "I'm glad she waited until now."

Starr nodded and closed her eyes to his gaze. She was glad, was truly thankful for what she and Shane had just shared. But she wondered if it had been wise, wondered what it had accomplished, except to bring them both incredible pleasure, wondered how she was going to live without him.

When Trixie's howls grew louder, Shane slid to his side, then to his feet. Starr pulled on her jeans, searched for her shirt. She bent to retrieve it from the floor, but before she'd slipped it over her head, Shane's arm encircled her from behind. Starr went still, pressing her back against his bare chest. Neither said a word, and the moment took on an ethereal quality accompanied by the dog's suffering yowls.

"What did Mick want you to tell me?" he whispered.

Uncle Mick. The reason for her visit. The reason for Shane's presence in Pinesburg, in her life.

She stepped away from him, shrugged into her shirt, and told Trixie to hush before replying. "He'd like you to come by for supper tomorrow night."

"Will you be there?" he asked.

"For a few more days," she replied.

He seemed to digest her words carefully, studying her expression for hidden meaning. She pulled her gaze from his, looking at the open trunk at her feet.

Trixie let out three short yips, reminding Starr of her presence. "I'll tell Uncle Mick you'll join him. Six o'clock?"

"Six o'clock. I'll see *you* then."

She slid out the door, taking Trixie's leash in hand, without a backward glance, without a parting touch, without another word.

TWELVE

Silver moonbeams shone through the darkness, lighting her way along the curving path. Wispy ribbons of fog were already beginning to form, reminding Starr of the weather forecast she'd heard earlier that afternoon, when Mick had been asleep in his chair, and she and Shane had made love.

She knew she shouldn't be here. She'd *promised* Shane she wouldn't come near the lighthouse alone. But she'd *had* to come tonight. It was the only place she could go, the only place she could think, the only place she could remember.

Starr didn't go inside the lighthouse, but stood in the shadows of the trees, gazing at it in the moonlight. Memories washed over her. Memories of a ten-year-old girl with sad eyes, learning to laugh and play along the water's edge. Memories of a teenager, coming to grips with her new femininity. Memories of Uncle Mick, his warm brown eyes, his goodness and laughter.

Memories of serious brown eyes meeting hers across a room, of half smiles and rusty laughter, of masculine scents and textures, of melting at a special man's touch and coming apart in his arms. Memories of Shane.

Before new tears could fall, a movement far in the distance caught her attention. Backing up against a tree, Starr stood statue still. And waited.

Without the use of lights, a boat chugged to shore where the engine was cut. A few minutes later another boat joined the first. They were getting braver, or more stupid, because this time they didn't row to shore, didn't seem to be afraid of alerting someone to their arrival by the sounds of their engines.

The shadowed figures of two men, one carrying a crate, came ashore, then disappeared inside the lighthouse. Huddled beneath the tall pines, Starr didn't know what to do. She wished Shane was there with her. He'd know what to do.

As more ribbons of fog swirled above her head, one of the men hurried through the darkness, then boarded his boat. A moment later the engine sputtered to life and he left the shore.

Suddenly another man appeared from the shadows. With the ease of a spring breeze, this man sprinted to the other boat. Starr's heart rose to her throat. She'd recognize that physique, that economy of movement, anywhere. *Oh, Shane!*

Casting a quick look over his shoulder he waded into the water. With strength, agility, and speed, he climbed into the boat. A heartbeat later the engine sprang to life.

Just then the first man who'd arrived on shore came running from the lighthouse. Starr realized he was the same man they'd seen here last week. Moonlight glinted off his silver hair and the object he carried in his right hand. Starr gasped as two shots split the foggy silence. Panic welled within her as she strained to see whether either bullet had hit its target. The boat sped away. Shane was apparently unharmed. He took off across the lake.

With jerky movements the man ran to the water's edge, then surveyed the surrounding area. Something hadn't gone right. That something was Shane. He'd taken off in pursuit of the other man, stranding this person on shore.

Fear gripped her heart. Fear for her safety and for Shane's. He, a man who'd left his undercover work because he felt he'd lost the ability to deal with danger, who felt he'd let his young friend down, who'd lost faith in himself as a *man,* was risking his very life.

Would the man she loved drown in the very waters that claimed her parents' lives? The mere possibility was a painful stab in her heart.

With watchful eyes, Starr fixed her gaze on the stranger peering into the shadows where she stood. Her heartbeat obliterated the sound of waves slapping the shore. Not a single muscle moved. Only her mind raced ahead. She had no weapon, no means of protection. But she had an intimate knowledge of the area. She knew every trail, every tree, every clearing. If he continued toward her, she'd outwit him, lose him along the way.

Instead of choosing *her* trail, the man looked all around him. With worried, unsure movements he slithered into the shadows of the lighthouse, then beyond, toward the gate that led to the main road. A moment later he was out of sight.

Starr wasn't aware she'd held her breath until she released it in a long, ragged sigh. Her lungs ached from the pressure and from fear. That fear made her a prisoner of the shadows.

Heavy fog seemed to roll down from the heavens. *No*, she screamed silently. Shane will never be able to find his way back through dense fog. She remembered Uncle Mick's tales of ships completely lost in the milky whiteness of fogs such as this.

Her muscles were stiff with tension and the struggle of remaining perfectly still. Her eyes scanned the place she'd last seen the intruder and her ears strained to hear any strange sound.

The only sounds were the breaking waves on Lake Michigan. All she could see was swirling fog and the lighthouse tower. The tower. She'd light the lamp in the lighthouse. Starr cast a look all around her. What if the stranger hadn't left the property? What if he were hiding in the shadows? Watching. Waiting.

She took a deep breath. If she didn't get her pulse rate under control, her thundering heartbeat would lead him to her like radar. Her eyes scanned the surrounding area as she began to count. *One-Mississippi, two-Mississippi, three-Mississippi*. When she'd reached ten-Mississippi, she gulped in one last deep breath, then darted toward the lighthouse door.

Breathing heavily, she pressed her body against the old wood and surveyed the area around her. No one appeared to be trying to stop her.

Without her turning the knob, the door opened on silent hinges. Starr pressed her hand to her mouth to keep from screaming in fright. She swallowed her fear, then shut the door behind her.

Pitch blackness completely blinded her. At least

outside the fog had cloaked the air in white. Here, inside, there was nothing. Not a shard of light. Starr had never felt such panic. Like a blind woman, she reached her hands through the air, feeling for obstacles as she made her way toward the steps.

She navigated the spiraling stairs, then felt for her bearings when she reached the top. *Please, let there be oil for the lamp.* She wondered how long it had been since Uncle Mick had lit the signal.

Her fingers came into contact with the Fresnel lens which would revolve around the lamp by means of a clocklike device, greatly intensifying the beam of light. For the first time in her life, she wished the signal were automated, wished with all her might this light was modern, more powerful.

But wishing never made it so. If Starr knew anything at all, she knew that. People made things happen. Not wishes.

She felt for the wick, then unscrewed a cap and doused the wick in lamp oil. Matches. She'd need matches to light it! Starr groped through her deep pockets, fumbling over a paper clip, two tissues, a button, candy bar wrappers, and several items she couldn't identify. After frantic seconds spent searching, she pulled a Main Street Café matchbook from the pocket. Just in case there really were lucky stars, Starr thanked them now.

The match shivered to life in the darkness. She touched it to the wick which burst into bright flames. She wound the mechanism which made the light appear to flash on and off, then hurried back down the stairs. If the light could guide Shane to safety, it could also bring the intruder back to investigate.

Once again Starr huddled beneath the trees at the

edge of the lighthouse property to watch and wait. The signal flashed through the fog as her pulse strummed beneath the thin skin at her wrists.

She had no idea how long she stood there. She was only aware that the flashing signal was Shane's only hope of finding his way back home.

The boat's engine had covered the sound of the shot, but Shane heard the bullet whiz past him, felt the air current brush his temple. These men were armed. Dangerous. His pulse thudded in his ears and he crouched lower in the boat.

At first the light from the full moon had lit his way across the lake. But swirling ribbons of fog gathered to form sheets, blocking the moonlight from view for longer and longer stretches. Shane squinted against the darkness, barely able to keep the other boat in view. The other vessel had turned its light on a mile back but Shane continued on in darkness.

Beads of sweat broke out on his upper lip in spite of the cold night air. Shane watched as the boat headlights shone on a dark mass up ahead. It was an island. He cut his engine and drifted, keeping the vessel in view.

The boat neared the island shore, then the man turned off his engine, thereby cutting off the only source of light. Shane could only guess what the man was doing. He crouched low in his boat as it drifted toward the island. For a moment the fog swirled to allow a single moonbeam to penetrate the darkness. In that moment he saw a man standing on a dock, peering out at the lake.

Shane stayed low until he'd rounded a bend, hoping he hadn't been spotted. He then dropped the anchor near shore, leaving no slack in the rope, and waded through the water. At the water's edge, he watched and listened. Wind whispered through the trees. Waves lapped the shore. His blood rushed through his body.

The dock was now empty.

A sixth sense, a premonition, the rustle of a pebble skittering through sand, alerted Shane. He lunged to the side and swung around. *Whoosh!* A club cut through the air, missing his head by a fraction of an inch.

He dodged another blow. Then another. He grabbed a piece of driftwood to use as a shield, then rushed the man. He brought the shield up, swift and hard, knocking the club from the man's hand.

Shane felt blinded in the foggy darkness, relying on sound and instinct. A fist came out of nowhere and caught him in the stomach. His makeshift shield thudded to the sand.

His own fist *thwacked* as it made contact with his opponent's nose. Without warning Shane jabbed him in the stomach. The man cried out in pain, then fell to his knees.

Shane didn't wait for another round. Instead, he took off down the dock where he landed inside the boat in one long leap. The engine sputtered to life and Shane untied the rope and sped away from the dock a moment before the other man arrived at the water's edge.

Without turning on the lights, Shane swooped around the point where he'd "parked" the boat he'd come in. It was becoming more difficult to see in the thickening fog. He brought one boat alongside the other, grasped the anchor rope, tied it securely, then took off in the direction he'd come, towing the second boat behind him.

Once he was a safe distance from the island, he flipped on the high-powered light. Peering all around him, he realized the sound he heard was his own stampeding heartbeat. Grooves cut into his face; tension cut into his chest. He remembered all too vividly why he'd left Chicago.

Not a beam of natural light penetrated the fog. The moon had been full earlier. Now there was only darkness. At that moment he'd have sold his very soul for the light of one bright star.

The headlights did little good. They didn't penetrate more than a few yards ahead. White swirled in every direction except down, and down there was only the blackness of Lake Michigan.

Minutes passed. Shane had no idea how many. He also had no idea he was even heading in the right direction. He was lost in. a sea of swirling white and great rolling waves of black. Using the boat's compass, he pressed on, hoping he was heading toward home.

He blinked. A speck, like a tiny firefly, flashed in the distance. He blinked again, afraid to trust his eyes. As the faint light continued to beckon, the tension in his gut lessened and he adjusted the angle of the wheel, turning the boat in the direction of that tiny light.

He'd wished for the light of one bright star. As Shane pushed up on the throttle, speeding through the midnight gloom toward his guiding light, he realized it had been a long, long time since his wishes had come true.

THIRTEEN

Beams of light slashed the darkness. Starr had no idea how long it had been since she'd lit the signal in the lighthouse. Time wasn't marked by seconds, but by bright flashes of light.

Her back was ramrod straight, her arms folded in front of her. Her heart beat a fast gallop beneath her palm. In her other hand she gently traced the peace signs dangling from the chain at her neck. A new kind of fear had settled over her. She was no longer afraid of being alone. Now she was afraid for Shane's life. She'd struck a deal with the stars, made a pact with the spirit high above them.

Her heart was filled to overflowing with love for Shane and Uncle Mick and the people in this town. She'd done all she could to guide Shane to safety. Now it was up to the heavens and if they saw fit to bring him back, she'd welcome him home, then give him her ultimate gift. She'd return to New York, to allow Shane and his grandfather time to get to know one another.

A siren echoed eerily through the distance, increasing in volume as it neared. Blue light flashed ever closer, then stopped at the gate.

Starr remained hidden in the shadows.

"Lass!" A deep voice rang out through the fog. "Lass, where are you?"

"Here, Uncle Mick. I'm here."

Trixie came bounding toward her as Mick and Maybell stepped from the police car. With a new spring to his step, her uncle followed Trixie's exuberant barks.

Starr hurried to meet him. "Uncle Mick, how did you know I was here?"

She noted the pleased, excited expression on his face. "Who else would have lit the signal in our tower?"

He'd said *our*. It warmed her heart.

"Mick and I and Trixie here just captured us a crook," Maybell declared.

"You what?" Starr cried. "But how? When I left, you were sound asleep, Uncle Mick."

"Sometime after you left, Trixie here let out a howl that could have woke the dead. She knew somethin' was goin' on, lass, so I put her on her leash and took her outside. Maybell was just coming up the walk. She'd been listening to her police scanner—"

"Someone reported shots fired near the old lighthouse," May interrupted. "I rushed to tell Mick."

Starr looked from May's bright eyes to Mick's smug expression. Mick pointed to the police car where two county deputies were guarding a man wearing handcuffs, the same man she'd seen earlier entering the lighthouse carrying a crate, the man with the silver ponytail.

"Mick and I were going back to my place to listen to the scanner. We were in the alley behind the store when a police car went flying by, his siren wailin', his flashers beaming. A stranger with a silver pony-tail ducked into the alley—"

Mick interrupted May's tale. "Maybell had told me you and Shane were askin' questions about a man fittin' his description. Before I could decide what to do, Trixie jerked from my grasp and lunged for the man. The streetlight out front cast shadows across the alley and when that man stepped from one of those shadows, he was aiming his gun right at poor Trixie and I figured there was only one reason why a stranger would be runnin' from the police, carrying a gun."

"He acted as if he was enjoying scaring the livin' daylights out of that dog, Starr," Maybell gushed. "I'm telling you, I was scared to death, land sakes, I was. Trixie just kept on backing away from him. The man took a step toward her, then another."

"When he slunk past me, I tripped him with my cane. For some reason he thought it was a shotgun," Mick declared.

"Could be because you told him to lie still or you'd blast him," Maybell explained.

Mick's eyes twinkled with new vitality. "Then Trixie and I stood guard while May went to get help."

Maybell clucked like a mother hen. "He lost his gun when he fell so I picked it up for safekeeping. You know how Trixie dislikes certain men. She got a hold of the seat of his pants. The man didn't dare move."

Starr shook her head and breathed a sigh of relief

that Uncle Mick was all right. Her relief wouldn't be complete until Shane was safely ashore.

"Where's Shane, lass?"

"He's out there." Starr pointed toward Lake Michigan. "He took off after another man."

"Land sakes," Maybell gushed. "I figured you and Shane were up to something when you came by asking questions about strangers in the area, but I never dreamed there would be shots fired near our village."

A heavy weight settled to Starr's stomach. Shane was still out there. Somewhere. Alive. Or dead. A raw, heartfelt sense of grief nearly overwhelmed her. She turned to gaze at the water, as if she could will him to see the lighthouse signal.

A fleshy arm came around her shoulders and she was pulled against Maybell's side. "The love shining from your eyes alone would be enough to guide him home. He'll make it back, Starr. Didn't I tell you a man is no match for a woman in love?"

Starr's gaze clouded with tears. Those tears seemed to magnify a quivering light far in the distance. She swiped at them, fearing it was nothing but a mirage.

But the light came steadily closer, growing brighter with every heartbeat. Uncle Mick's voice came from behind her. Car doors slammed. Other voices called to each other in the night. Starr barely registered these sounds, so tuned was her attention to that shimmering light. She hurried to the water's edge, Mick and Maybell close behind. A moment later the boat came into view, towing another.

He cut the engine and a cheer went up. Starr looked around her at the gathering crowd. It seemed half the town had turned out for the excitement.

Shane threw down the anchor, then jumped to the shore. He landed on both feet, but Starr had seen him wince in pain. Before he said a word, his eyes searched the crowd for her.

The lighthouse signal pulsated through the night. Blue light flashed from the police cars. Fog swirled all around them. For interminable seconds Shane gazed into her eyes. Relief flooded her senses, and she smiled.

Something invisible seemed to flicker through the air between them. Shane answered her smile with one of his own, that half smile she'd come to crave.

The crowd quieted, straining to hear what was going on. Starr and Shane were questioned. Mick and Maybell retold the story of their already famous capture. A deputy cut through the people, making his way to the sheriff's car where he put out a call to the Coast Guard to pick up the man Shane had stranded on the island. The sheriff asked Shane to come back to the station with him and Starr turned to take Uncle Mick home.

A gentle nudge had her looking over her shoulder. Shane's warm hand gripped hers and she found herself gazing into his eyes. "This may take a while, but when I'm through, *we* have a lot to talk about."

"I'll be waiting." She'd wait for him all night, if necessary. There were so many things she needed to tell him. When she was through, she'd tell him goodbye.

He squeezed her hand, rubbing his thumb across the sensitive skin at her wrist. She watched him go, watched him settle himself inside the sheriff's car. He'd always been a handsome devil; now he was a self-confident one, too.

*   *   *

Hours later Uncle Mick's snores permeated the silence. Starr dodged the louder creaks in the linoleum as she had countless times before. But this time was different. This time *she* was different. So many changes had taken place in so short a time. She'd never seen Uncle Mick so happy, so proud. She couldn't remember a time when the town had turned out in the middle of the night to cheer for one of their own.

Changes were everywhere. And they all centered around Shane. Uncle Mick was well on his way to recovering from his stroke. There was a new spring to his step that had nothing to do with physical therapy. Mick's questions and misgivings about Hannah's love had been answered. He finally understood why she'd married his best friend, why they'd had a child, his child. Because of Shane's search, Mick had found his grandson, a man of his own blood.

But most of all, Shane had changed her. A new peacefulness filled her heart. She loved him. And she was happy for him, for Mick, for the town. If that peacefulness was edged with sadness, she'd learn to live with it.

A light knock on the door had her hurrying through the stillness to greet Shane. Instead of Shane, she opened the door to her best friend. "Joanna! What are you doing here?"

"I was up with the baby when I heard the sirens. Maybell saw the light and stopped by to tell me what had happened and I had to come here myself to make sure you're all right."

Starr smiled indulgently at her friend's ramblings. "I'm glad you stopped by, Jo. I was going to come by later to say good-bye and to see Jenny and Sydney before I leave.''

"Before you leave? But why? I thought you'd stay this time.''

"I have to work." Starr's gaze slid from Joanna's shrewd look.

"You could get a job at the hospital here.''

"Shane deserves time to get to know his grandfather." How could she tell her friend she was leaving out of love?

Joanna narrowed her eyes and Starr felt like she'd just been caught snitching a candy bar minutes before supper. "You and Jenny!" Jo shook her head. "Neither of you realizes love isn't confined to the size of our hearts. Our love for Jenny hasn't diminished because we now have two children to love. Starr, Mick's love for you won't diminish simply because he now has a grandson.''

"I know. But it isn't just the love, Jo. They're *family*.''

Dawn streaked the sky with pale periwinkle, lavender, and coral. Walking toward the lighthouse, Starr looked from the fog-misted colors in the east to the still slumbering sky in the west.

The lighthouse lay somewhere in between.

Once again the door opened on silent hinges and Starr remembered the fear that had nearly burst her lungs when she'd opened it in total darkness a matter of a few hours ago. Fear had driven her then, fear for Shane's safety. Now she was bone tired, but too restless to sleep.

She pushed her hair behind her shoulders, then quietly walked up the stairs. From the top step she stared into the distance where Lake Michigan lay in early dawn. She was going to miss this view. She was going to miss this town and its people. But not as much as she was going to miss Shane.

He'd said, when I'm through, we have to talk. She'd waited all night but he hadn't come. She hadn't seen him since he'd driven away in the sheriff's car. Saying good-bye wasn't going to be easy.

Not a sound was heard, not a word was spoken, yet Starr knew Shane was there. She turned, first her head, and then her entire body. Like the first time she'd met him in this very tower, she found herself gazing into Shane's intense brown eyes. This time she wasn't afraid. He was no longer a stranger to her.

"How do you do that?" she asked.

"Do what?" His voice was deep and smooth.

"Move without making a sound."

He shrugged and stepped closer. "I went to Mick's first. When you weren't there I knew I'd find you here."

"I waited all night, Shane."

"So have I, Starr." She didn't understand the intense look in his eyes and decided fatigue was probably clouding her thought processes.

"These small towns use as many forms as the big ones," he murmured as he took another step, never taking his eyes from her.

"Do they?" She watched as he reached into his pocket, remembering the first time she'd met him, when she'd been afraid he was reaching for a weapon. This time, as before, he brought out a brown wrapper.

He inclined his head and raised his eyebrows. She

accepted one light brown candy, then stared deep into his eyes. "You're a hero, Shane. People around here will never forget last night. Mick's proud as punch."

She glanced away, then down at her hand. The milk chocolate candy was melting fast. Shane brought her hand to his lips, then took the candy into his mouth, touching his tongue to the chocolate melting on her palm. Starr closed her eyes, her heart melting faster than the candy.

When she opened them, she found him watching her, a glint lighting his gaze. "I haven't had a chance to thank you, Starr."

"Thank me? You're the hero."

"Your light led me home."

His words swelled her heart; his nearness melted her senses. "I'm glad you're safe, Shane." She quickly added, "We all are," then floundered beneath his gaze.

Looking away, into the distant view, she asked, "What were those men doing in this lighthouse?"

Shane raked his hair off his forehead before answering. "It took most of the night to get a straight answer. The Coast Guard captured the man I stranded on that island. He refused to talk at all. But the one Mick and Maybell captured finally listened to reason."

Starr could imagine Shane making criminals see reason. He leaned against a window frame, his back to the view. She saw weariness on his features, in his stance. It had been a long night for them both.

"When I took those old spectacles we'd found on the shore to Chicago, I had them analyzed. They were old, but weren't scratched. So they couldn't have washed up on shore. That had to mean someone *dropped* them there.''

''Who?'' she asked.

''Those intruders in this lighthouse. Mick's talked of ships wrecked in winter storms here in the Great Lakes. Those men were using this lighthouse as a meeting place to smuggle artifacts from Lake Michigan.''

''Smuggling old spectacles?'' she asked.

''And gold, copper, silver, brass, antiques, anything of value. Shipwrecks are underwater preserves. Divers need permits to remove anything from a sunken ship. And these guys didn't have any permit, believe me.''

Starr walked to the vast windows overlooking the lake. In a few hours the sun would burn off the fog, brighten another day. In a few hours she'd be on her way to New York.

''You accomplished everything you came here to do, Shane. And then some.'' He'd come here to find his answers and he'd ended up capturing criminals. ''And so have I.'' She came here to help Uncle Mick regain his strength, and ended up falling in love.

''I'm going back to New York. I'm leaving later today.'' She hoped he didn't notice the forced brightness in her voice.

''So am I.''

Her emotions reeled with confusion. ''But why? You're only beginning to know Uncle Mick. And you said you have no reason to return to Chicago. Why not stay here?''

''I'm going to New York. With you. I love you, Starr.''

Her mind refused to form coherent thoughts. She

didn't know what to say. Shane slid his hands up her arms to her shoulders, lightly skimming her neck, her face. "You give and give and give. But you never ask for anything in return. What do *you* want, Starr?"

She looked away, but he brought her chin up. The lines in his face deepened. "All right, I'll guess. You want to live here, in this village."

"Yes."

"You want to be near Mick and Joanna and Maybell and Trixie."

When she didn't answer, he continued. "You want a home of your own, and a couple of kids."

"Six." A smile started at the corners of her mouth.

"Six?" His mouth twitched.

She only nodded. If she ever had children they'd never be lonely, never feel totally alone.

"I love you," he murmured. "And we'd better get started." His arms came around her, pulling her into his strong embrace. His lips teased her, from her forehead all the way down to her chin.

"What?" she gasped.

"We'd better get started if you want six kids." He grinned, he actually grinned.

"Not about that. What did you say before that? Before you started talking about children. About following me to New York." *About loving me*, she added to herself.

Shane was silent as he tried to remember what he'd said, what she didn't understand. "I love you, Starr. Your eyes have been telling me what you won't say. Until last night, I didn't recognize their message. You love me. Will you marry me, Starr?"

He loved her. She believed it with all her heart. He'd follow her to New York if she asked him to, leaving Uncle Mick, his grandfather, the man he'd come here to find.

She rose on tiptoe to capture his lips with her own. When the kiss ended, she murmured, "I love you, Shane Wells." A shiver of wanting ran through her as he lowered her to the floor. She touched him through his clothing, her urgency matching his.

"And you'll marry me?" he asked against her lips.

"Yes." Starr whispered his name between kisses, her voice catching on the depth of her feelings for this man.

"The sheriff offered me a job last night," he murmured against her ear.

"Did you accept?"

"I told him I'd let him know. I've been thinking, Starr. How would you like to modernize the lighthouse cottage? It's going to need a sizable addition if we're going to have six kids. Which brings me back to this. Any suggestions as to ways to begin the first of those six children?"

"Suggestions?" she whispered. "I might have a few." She pulled his face down to hers and kissed him. Her hands roamed down his body, seeking pleasure, and giving it. When he moaned her name, she forgot to answer with words, letting her body speak to his.

Dust particles twinkled through the air. Outside, waves lapped the shore of the Great Lake. Inside, Starr murmured Shane's name. He returned her love, kiss for kiss, breath for breath, heartbeat for heartbeat. In their own way they answered each other. After all, they never had answered with words.

EPILOGUE

The spicy aroma of roasting pig hung thick on the muggy air along with bits of conversations and children's laughter. Starr's footsteps were brisk as her gaze searched the water's edge, the sandy shoreline, the stand of pines.

"Land sakes, Starr, you look like you've seen a ghost," Maybell gushed.

Her heart rate returned to normal and a smile lifted her lips. "Not a ghost, May. For a minute I lost sight of the twins."

Maybell followed Starr's line of vision and tut-tutted as she scolded, "Those two keep you hoppin', land sakes they do. I do declare little Jazz is as cantankerous as his great-grandpa. I'd say you deserve it for giving him a name the likes of Jazz. And Jake's never far behind. Honestly, Starr, I don't know how you do it."

Love as big as Lake Michigan filled her chest as she murmured, "Excuse me a minute, May." Her steps took her past the marigolds blooming by the back step, past the curving brick walkway, and beyond the tiny garden, her gaze never straying from the sight of Shane. Having just come off duty, he still wore his deputy's uniform, and if she lived to be a hundred, she'd never tire of looking at him, in uniform or wearing nothing at all.

He carried three-year-old Jazz like a sack of potatoes over his shoulder and held Jake tight to his side beneath his arm. Or was it the other way around? From this distance, Starr couldn't be sure.

She knew the exact moment he noticed her. Their gazes met and everything else went still. A Mona Lisa smile lifted her lips as she strolled to his side. She reached for the twin nearest her, who turned out to be Jazz, not Jake as she'd first thought. She raised her mouth for Shane's kiss, then kissed each of the boys' smooth cheeks before setting them on the grass at their feet. Trixie kept them corralled like lambs, the boys' giggles blending with party noises.

"I missed you," she murmured. She always missed him when it was his turn to work the night shift. She missed him in their bed, she missed his warmth, his touch.

"And I, you," he murmured in her ear, his breath tickling her temple, his lips brushing her cheek.

Trixie chose that moment to bark, and Shane scowled at the animal. "Blasted dog. She never has let me kiss you. It's just a good thing Mick wanted her, or we'd have a terrible time filling all the new rooms in that house." He pointed to their home, to the sizeable addition, the vast windows facing the Great Lake.

"Where there's a will, there's a way," she teased.

The child growing beneath her heart chose that moment to do a fast flutter kick against Starr's abdomen. She took Shane's large hand in hers and placed it on the swell of her stomach. "Do you feel that?"

A look of wonder shone from his eyes, and a smile pulled at his mouth, the grooves at each corner barely more than a memory.

"What do you think of the name Hannah?" she asked.

"A girl this time?"

She nodded, taking a sheet of paper from her pocket and handing it to him. "We can put her first photo in the trunk along with her grandmother Hannah's and right next to little Jake's and Jazz's, and the pictures of the wonderful people for whom they're named."

Shane studied the bloblike image, which to him looked as if someone had squashed peanut butter and jelly between two sheets of paper and made a copy of it. He turned it, first one way, then the other, trying to understand how a technician could be certain the image was even a baby, let alone a baby girl.

"Just one this time?" he asked.

"Hallelujah," she replied.

As if drawn to the warmth of her father's hand, the baby rolled and kicked. Feeling his child move inside Starr never ceased to move him. He fought the desire to let his hand roam lower, to bring his other hand to her breast.

Love was mirrored in her eyes; so was desire. He saw wishes flit across her irises, wishes he'd make certain would come true. "Later," he promised.

"Yes," she agreed.

The twins ran ahead, Starr and Shane strolling leisurely behind toward the guests fast arriving or sitting on picnic tables beneath brightly colored umbrellas or sitting on the wide front porch or standing around the roasting pit where a whole hog turned slowly on a rotisserie.

Children ducked around adults, shrieking as they played. Mick stood watch over the entire group, his eyes full of pride as his gaze rested on Starr and Shane, then surreptitiously on each of the other guests. He'd been happier these past four years, happier than Starr had ever seen him. He claimed it had to do with his complete recovery from his stroke. Starr knew it had to do with Shane, and with the knowledge that Hannah *had* loved him. So had Jake.

"You realize if we name this child Hannah, we'll have to have another to name after Mick," Shane teased.

"I don't mind," she answered. "After all, we always said we wanted six." Mick had been adamant about naming their *last* child, boy or girl, after him. Not their first.

From her distance, Starr grinned as she watched Joanna abruptly change direction the moment she noticed Maybell in her path. Upon reaching Starr's side, Jo breathed a sigh of relief. "Whew. That was close."

Starr laughed, and Joanna smiled in spite of herself. Her relief was short-lived, though, because minutes later Maybell clucked like a mother hen. "Joanna, your Sydney just tripped little Amy Parker."

Joanna cast a look in Starr's direction, then went in search of her younger daughter. Maybell made a show of looking the whole scene over before saying, "Land sakes, Starr, this town's growin' right before my very eyes, what with you and Joanna both expecting another baby and nearly every other able-bodied woman, too. It was that cold winter we had, I'm tellin' you."

Starr gazed into Shane's eyes. She knew it was more than the cold winter. It was the love in her husband's eyes, the warmth in his touch, the rusty laughter that tumbled from him when she least expected. It was the man, the sense of belonging his arms promised, the sense of rightness she felt each time she answered his touch with her own.

Sturdy tables were set up, enough food to feed a small army set out, plates filled, glasses drained. For the fourth year in a row, Starr and Shane's Fourth of July party was a huge success. The pink and yellow and orange sunset streaked the sky, then darkness gradually fell. The lighthouse lamp was lit, the flashing signal holding the night at bay.

Sprawled on blankets on the grass, Jazz fell asleep in Starr's lap, Jake on Shane's shoulder, both oblivious of the fireworks bursting in the sky, of the *oohs* and *ahs* following each display.

Shane took a bite of chocolate, then handed the bar to Starr. As sweet chocolate and caramel melted over her taste buds, her gaze locked with his. Fireworks burst overhead, rockets boomed from the ground. Voices rose and fell and one corner of his mouth lifted in that seductive way that made her forget where she was, forget she was six months' pregnant with their third child, forget everything except the promise in her husband's eyes.

This was truly her town, and his. Their roots went

as deep as Lake Michigan, their love even deeper. The lighthouse signal reminded her of that night so long ago when she'd waited in fear for his safe return. Each year they lit the signal; each year she thanked her lucky stars for guiding him home. To her.

Soon the guests would go home, and she and Shane would leave the light in the tower burning, flashing through the darkness. They'd tuck the boys into their beds, their eyes would meet, their hearts full, desire heavy in their chests, as heavy as the muggy July night. No matter how dark the night, how deep the darkness, in each other's arms they'd find light, in each other's arms they'd hold back the night, and their most secret wishes would come true.